THE LABRADOR

AND

THE POCKET WATCH

PINEWOOD MYSTERY

T. BROWN

ISBN : 979-8-9904693-0-3

The Labrador and The Pocket Watch

Books by T Brown

Pinewood Mystery Series

The Labrador and the Pocket Watch ©2021

The Labrador and the Pocket Watch revised edition ©2024.

Never in my wildest dreams did I think I would be writing a mystery series, let alone dedicating a book to a dog!

This book is dedicated to Trick, a big lovable black Labrador, who comes to visit me at least twice a week, until I take him home in the 'Trick Taxi' a.k.a. my vehicle. He inspired this book with his visits and my imagination.

Emma Johnson had moved to the small town of Pinewood, in East Texas, ten years ago. She made the move shortly after beginning a new career, writing children's books. She had grown tired of the fast-paced life of living in a big city. So, when she decided to move, what better place then closer to family.

She decided on the small town where her daughter and son-in-law, Shelby and Tim, had been living for twelve years. Tim had grown up in the area, so a year after they got married, they moved to Pinewood.

She was lucky enough to find her small dream house with a wraparound porch and a porch swing looking out over the lake.

Shelby and Tim live across the lake from Emma with their two dogs, a black Labrador named Charlie, and his sidekick Dash, a blue heeler.

They love the small town with a population of approximately two hundred. Shelby owns the Brewin' n' Bakin' Coffee Shop which has a patio overlooking the lake. Tim owns the Cast-A-Line bait and tackle shop next door.

Even though Pinewood is off the beaten path, it does have a State Highway that is also the main street through town. Due to the traffic, they have two successful businesses.

People from other neighboring towns as well as those passing through stop at the coffee shop for a slice of Shelby's specialty, sopapilla cheesecake.

Tim stays busy with the bait shop through the spring and summer months and then closes up shop the first of October for the season. He then helps Shelby out at the coffee shop.

Although it is a small community, there is a family style restaurant, a few other small shops, a gas station, as well as a small public library.

Emma's friend Mary Stuart runs the community library. Mary had been a librarian with the *Dallas Public Library* system before moving to the small town in East Texas. She has now been the head librarian at the Pinewood Public Library for a little over twenty years.

She and Emma became good friends shortly after Emma moved to the lake house. They both have a love for reading mysteries. They are close in age and have many of the same interests.

It is a lovely location in East Texas, with the beautiful pine trees and even more beautiful sunsets over the lake.

The bigger city of White Rock is only sixty

miles away, with plenty of shopping opportunities. It is also where Emma's longtime friend, Detective Alex Day works at the County Sheriff's office.

They had met in 2005 when she was on a wildland fire assignment as the Public Relations Officer. They have been good friends ever since.

Alex has never been married and Emma has been divorced since 2004. They had hit it off from their first meeting. However, it has never been more than a good friendship and that is how it will remain.

Emma and her Pitbull, Sam, loves the small-town life, and she stays busy with her writing of children's books. Although she is not a 'best' selling author, it does pay the bills.

She enjoys writing , and she can do it all online from publishing to sales. Working from home suits her well.

A few years after Emma moved in, her daughter's black Labrador figured out on his own how to get to her house.

He started coming to visit a couple of times a week. Of course, Charlie also knows that he will get to go for a ride when Emma takes him home.

Over the years, Charlie has brought her 'trinkets' he has found, and soon they were 'communicating'.

Emma learned that when he paws her shoulder from the backseat, he wants her to stop and let him out. He usually leads her to wherever he has found something.

A few times it has turned out to be helpful in cases of stolen or missing property that the sheriff's department was investigating.

Five years ago, was when Emma decided

to get a pup of her own. A black and white Pitbull, that she named Sam. She found him at the animal shelter in White Rock. As soon as she met Sam, she adopted him. He was only a few months old.

Charlie and Sam became good buddies and enjoy running around the yard and playing together. Sam also knows when Emma is not paying attention and barks at her when he sees his buddy coming.

It is a nice start to September, shaping up to be a beautiful day in East Texas. Emma is contentedly enjoying her morning coffee while sitting on the porch swing. Sam is laying at her feet as she checks her email.

Suddenly Sam jumps up and begins barking, Emma looks up from her laptop and just as she expected, here comes Charlie _______ with something in his mouth.

He drops it at the top of the steps and takes off chasing Sam around the yard. Emma shakes her head. She sets her coffee cup down, places her laptop on the swing next to where she is sitting. She walks over to see what he has left her this time.

It is an old-style man's hat, the kind she has seen in pictures of old magazines and in old movies. It is the type that newspaper boys once wore in the 1940's.

Emma thinks out load, "Where in the heck did this crazy dog come across this?"

He must have dug it up or found it in the nearby woods. It is very dirty and very faded.

She lays it aside, takes her coffee cup in and calls for Sam to come inside. Charlie knows that if Sam is going inside, playtime is over, and it is time for his ride home. He goes to wait for Emma by her SUV.

She tells Sam to be a good dog and she will be back in just a few minutes. After locking the front door, she opens the back door of her vehicle, and Charlie hops right in.

After starting her vehicle, she puts the back windows down for Charlie. He loves sticking his head out and sniffing the air.

As she nears the wooded area known for

the old Indian mounds (where arrow heads have been discovered) he paws her shoulder from the backseat. She knows what this means, he wants her to stop.

"Okay, I'm pulling over."

Emma pulls off on the side of the road and lets him out, he leads her to the area of the Indian mounds. Thinking he found the cap here, she takes a walk, looks around but does not see anything of interest.

She lets him snoop around as she sits on a fallen tree for a minute. She loves the peacefulness of the woods and the fresh air. It is so quiet and relaxing.

Charlie comes up and sits next to her, raising his paw to hold 'hands'. She pats him on the head, "Come on, time to get you home."

After dropping him off and telling him to stay home, she cannot help but wonder where he found the old cap. How had it ended up wherever he found it?

From the looks of it, it has not been worn in an awfully long time. It is so faded she cannot tell what the original color was as well as being very dirty.

Talking to herself, "I can't read too much into this he just dug it up somewhere. It likely belonged to some boy who lost it years ago."

A week later Charlie comes by for his usual visit, a little later in the day than normal.

This time he shows up with something metal hanging out the side of his mouth. He bounds up on the porch and lays it on her lap.

Emma pats his head, "Well what have you brought me this time?"

Charlie wags his tail and heads off into the yard to play with Sam. They immediately start playing tug-of-war with one of Sam's toys.

After dusting some of the dirt off, she realizes that it is an old pocket watch and chain. She takes it inside to get a soft rag and wipes off as much of the dirt as she can. When she turns it over and wipes the back, three engraved initials can be made out, B.L.T.

They had been completely hidden by the dirt stuck to it. She ponders over the initials but cannot think of anyone's name with those letters. She tucks the watch into a plastic baggie and puts it in her backpack.

She glances at the clock. It is time for Shelby and Tim to be home. She grabs her keys, loads Charlie up in her SUV and begins the drive to their house.

He starts whining, so she puts his window down. He immediately sticks his nose out and smells all the scents in the air.

Again, as she nears the area of the Indian mounds, he paws her shoulder and starts barking. She pulls over and opens the door to let him out, he immediately barks at her to follow him.

This time he leads her past the Indian mounds and to a nearby stock tank.

Being a year of drought in Texas, which is not anything out of the ordinary these past several years, the tank is almost completely dried up. She walks around the edge, seeing deer and raccoon tracks near what water is left.

She comes to an area that has been dug up. Due to the scratch marks in the dirt, she immediately determines that it must be where Charlie was digging and found the watch. He sniffs the area but quickly loses interest.

She does not find anything else, so she calls for him to come with her. As she pulls away, she looks in the rearview mirror and she sees him sitting there nobly.

"You know this is not your personal limo."

He cocks his head to the side, as if to say, "What do you mean, not my personal limo?" She cannot help but laugh at this silly dog.

She pulls in the driveway just as Tim and Shelby are getting out of their Jeep. As she opens her door, she hears Shelby call to Tim,

"Charlie's taxi is here."

"If he keeps this up, I am going to install a meter."

They are laughing as he puts his paw on Emma's hand. Tim unlocks the front door and Dash, the blue heeler, comes running out. Barking and fussing at Charlie as usual.

It is a nice cool mid-September morning when Charlie shows up for a visit, but he does not bring Emma any trinkets or prizes this time.

He has just come to play with Sam. After the dogs run around the yard for a while, she calls them up on the porch and gives them some dog treats.

She tells them to lay down while she finishes the last chapter of the mystery she has been reading. Sam lays on his blanket under the swing while Charlie curls up on the rug by the back door.

After finishing her book, she grabs her keys, backpack, and the other books to return to the library.

She puts Sam in his fenced yard and loads Charlie up for his ride home. After dropping him off, she tells him to stay home, and then she checks her watch. As she pulls away, she checks her mirror and sees that Charlie is curled up on the front porch.

Emma decides to stop off for a cup of coffee and a slice of cheesecake before heading to the library. Sounds like a good breakfast to her.

Tim is there having a glass of iced tea since business is beginning to slow down at the bait shop. It is getting to be that time of year _________ almost fall.

She tells them about the treasures that Charlie has brought her and shows them the watch. Since he is always digging something up, they do not pay much attention to it.

She finishes her coffee and tells them, "See y'all later" and heads off to the library.

Shelby turns to Tim, "She is doing it

again! You know she is more curious than she is letting on. I am sure this is going to lead to one of her adventures, as she calls it."

She clears the table, shaking her head, she knows her mother too well.

Tim looks out the window, "The watch is interesting. Why does our dog always take her his discoveries, instead of us?"

Tim heads back over to the bait shop, Shelby shakes her head as she watches him walk across the parking lot.

There are a few customers that have just pulled up. He recognizes the trucks, a couple of regular, local customers. He knows they are just stopping in for some bait and to share some tall tales of fishing in days gone by.

At this time of day, the library is not terribly busy, so it gives Emma the chance to show Mary the watch that Charlie brought to her.

As they visit and talk about the possibilities of where it could have come from, she shows Mary the initials on the back, B.L.T.

Mary sarcastically comments, "I don't think it stands for bacon, lettuce and tomato."

They both laugh at that as they discuss how old the watch might be. That is when it occurs to Emma that she will take it to Detective Day. He knows about antiques and collectibles like this watch. Maybe he can tell her more about it. Mary agrees that it might not be a bad idea.

Since she and Mary are both avid readers of mysteries, she is as intrigued by the items as Emma.

"There is no telling where it came from, or how long it has been out there in the woods, if that is where it was originally lost."

Emma replies, "It could have been lost by someone fishing in the tank years ago. Charlie just happen to find it because it is nearly dried up. I still don't know why he brings his treasures to me."

Emma pulls her books out of her backpack to turn them in. Which reminds Mary that she just got in a new shipment of mysteries. She pulls them from behind the counter and shows them to Emma.

She always holds back the new mysteries that come in until Emma has a chance to check them out. She chooses three of the new books and heads for home.

As she carries her backpack up the steps, she thinks aloud, "Like I really need more books to read. I need to finish writing my own book and get it to the publisher."

She sets her bag on the porch swing and lets Sam out of his yard. She gets her laptop out and works on some finishing touches on her new book.

Sam plays for a while and then joins her on the porch. He paws her leg and goes to the door, she knows what that means, he is ready for dinner. She fixes his bowl of food and heats herself up a bowl of soup in the microwave.

After finishing her dinner, she cleans up and fixes a cup of hot chocolate. She wipes down the counters and fixes her coffee pot for the next morning.

She grabs a new library book and heads over to the couch. Sam follows her and lays down on his bed.

She still cannot put the pocket watch out of her mind. She lays the book down, picks up her cell phone and calls Alex to see if he will be in his office tomorrow.

She tells him she has something old that she would like him to take a look at and see if there is anything he can tell her about it.

Alex rolls his eyes, wondering what Emma has come across now, or did that Labrador bring her something he dug up. He cannot believe the way she and that dog seem to communicate with each other.

"Drop by any time. I will be working at my office all day. Unless something unexpected comes up."

The next morning, she takes care of Sam, stops off at Brewin' n' Bakin' for a to-go cup of her favorite caramel coffee and heads for White Rock. She lets Shelby know that she is heading over to visit Alex.

"Actually, I'm taking the pocket watch for him to look at. I'm hoping he can tell me how old it is and any other information about it."

Shelby hands Emma her to go cup and tells her to have a safe drive.

As she is driving over, she notices the trees are just beginning to change colors, she loves the fall season. The leaves all in orange and reds, and the crisp, cool days. Spending time with Tim and Shelby, sitting around the fire pit.

She gets her mind back on driving and her

mission today. She is hoping that Alex can help her with information about the pocket watch, if anyone she knows can, it will be him. Detective Day welcomes her into his office.

"It's been a while since we had the chance to visit. How are things in your part of the world?"

She tells him she has been doing fine, almost finished working on her new book. But she needs his help with something.

Alex smiles and remarks, "Let me guess that black Lab brought you something."

She smiles as she reaches into her backpack and pulls out the baggie with the watch in it and lays it on Alex's desk.

"Is there anything you can tell me about this?"

He takes it out of the baggie, takes a good

look at it and gets up to retrieve a book from his collection he keeps in his office. He carefully opens the back of the watch, to discover the manufacturer and flips through the book.

Alex looks up at Emma and informs her that the watch was made by a small watch company in Kentucky. They were in business from 1850 to about 1875. It was not a high dollar watch to begin with, so the value of the watch now is not much. It is interesting, that it has initials engraved on it.

"I am not interested in how much it is worth. I was simply curious about how old it is."

"Well, even if it was made in their last year of business it would be about 145 years old."

He places the watch back in the baggie and hands it to Emma, she thanks him for the information and places it back in her backpack.

As she heads for the door, he tells her to stop by anytime, they can get together for lunch one day.

He realizes after she leaves his office she did not say where it came from. Of course, she does like finding odd items at junk stores. She picked it up at that little shop over in Pinewood.

He sits back down at his desk as Emma appears in his doorway. He looks up and smiles.

"You shouldn't stay away so long."

Emma rolls her eyes, "I forgot to mention where the watch came from."

She explains that Charlie brought it to her a few days ago. She describes where he led her, the wooded area where the Indian mounds are located.

"That's all I wanted to tell you, see ya later."

Alex smiles and leans back in his chair and thinks to himself, 'her and that dog'.

The next morning as Emma fixes the coffee pot and gets it brewing Sam begins barking at the backdoor.

She opens the door to let him out, and he bolts down the steps to greet his friend. She grabs a cup of coffee and her laptop and heads out to the porch swing.

The dogs are having a fun time running and playing in the yard. The cooler weather has them energized this morning. After she checks her email and updates her website, she decides to work on the new book she is writing.

She is having a tough time concentrating this morning. Between watching the dogs play and thinking about the items Charlie brought her.

She entertains the thought of writing a

mystery novel. It would be a new challenge, writing in a different genre. But, for now she dismisses that thought and goes back to editing her book.

After a few hours it is time for a break, and time to take Charlie home. She puts Sam into his fenced yard, loads Charlie in the SUV and heads for Shelby's house.

Being Sunday, she knows they will be home. When she pulls up and opens the back door for Charlie to get out, Dash comes running up to greet her and bark and fuss at his 'brother'. She notices that he has something stuck to the bottom of his back paw.

When she removes it, the dogs take off chasing each other. She looks at the piece of paper and realizes it is a piece of an old newspaper clipping. She dusts it off and tries to read it, but only parts of it are legible.

At the top of the piece of paper is a faded date. The only readable part is 'Novem' and the year, '1953'.

The only other part she can make out is part of the headline. Man missing ……… two weeks, and the name, Benjamin.

Is it just coincidence or does it have something to do with the cap and the watch? Maybe Benjamin is the B in B.L.T.

Her second thought is where did Dash come across this piece of newspaper? Unlike Charlie, he never tries to lead Emma to any specific area.

She does know that Dash does not stray extremely far from home. Although he has been known to go a little ways into the woods at the edge of Shelby and Tim's property.

Of course, a piece of paper could have

been blown there from anywhere. But a piece of newsprint ________ from 1953?

Shelby and Tim come out the front door. "Hi mom, are you running the taxi again?"

"Yes, he is probably tired now. He and Sam have been playing for about the past three hours."

Tim notices the piece of paper she is holding, and the quizzical look on her face.

"What do ya have there?"

She tells him it was stuck to Dash's paw and shows him that it is part of an old newspaper.

She tucks it in with the watch and puts it back into her backpack. If only it was not Sunday, she would stop off at the library and show it to Mary. Instead, she heads home, deciding to see if she can find anything on the internet pertaining to the old newspaper article.

After arriving back home she gets on her laptop, but instead of doing any research, she decides that she will work on her book. She would like to get it published in time for Christmas sales. She can do research later.

After a late lunch Emma and Sam head back out to the porch swing. She loves working outside and Sam likes to nap under the swing.

After working on her book and saving the final copy to her computer, she pats Sam and tells him, "Lets go inside and take a nap. We deserve a lazy Sunday afternoon."

Sam stretches and follows her inside. She gets the throw blanket and lays down on the couch with Sam cuddling against her legs.

After getting up from their nap, Emma lets Sam outside and fixes herself a cup of coffee. Emma hopes it kicks in quickly, she is just a tad groggy.

She lets Sam back inside, turns on the television, just for background noise. She decides to do some searching on the computer for missing persons in 1953.

She comes up empty handed. Of course, it is not like it would have been national news. It would not have even made it into the state news back then.

The next morning, after finishing her cup of coffee, she decides to put Sam in his fenced yard. Packs her backpack and heads to the library. Maybe Mary can help her find archives for newspapers from that year.

After about an hour, they cannot seem to

find anything online for archives of newspapers, at least not that far back. It makes it more difficult not knowing what newspaper it came from.

They agree, it had to be the newspaper in White Rock. It was the only newspaper in the county back then. Being that long ago it is not as if they had computers to store files on.

She decides that since it is still early in the day, she will drive over to White Rock. Maybe Alex has an idea about looking up the investigation for the missing person.

They had to file a report about him, he was missing for two weeks or longer.

After searching the records on his computer, he tells her, "The department records do not seem to go back that far. There could be some old files stored at the courthouse. But the chances are slim and none of unearthing them."

He does have an idea. He suggests that Emma should talk to a gentleman that lives just outside of Pinewood, Reuben Schmidt.

He tells her that he is very eccentric but a collector of books, newspapers, and other things. It is believed he is in his eighties, but he could be older.

Maybe he was around when the man went missing or has a copy of the newspaper for that date.

She tells Alex that she will think about it. She has driven by his place. It looks a little on the spooky side. Alex tells her to just be careful if she does decide to pay him a visit.

She stops off at the coffee shop when she arrives back in Pinewood. Tim has been helping since business has slowed down at the bait shop. They are not too busy, so Tim joins her for a cup of coffee. She tells him about her conversation with Alex.

As always Tim is a bit concerned, he is not too sure about her going out to visit Reuben Schmidt. He has heard about him and how he collects things, but he always keeps to himself.

He tells her to beware, Reuben has a large German Shepard and does not know how un-friendly it is. Having heard about Reuben, the dog is probably aggressive.

She assures Tim that she will be cautious if she decides to pay him a visit. She thinks to herself, 'he is just a lonely elderly man living alone for so many years.

From what she has heard prior to today, he never married, never really had any friends or relatives that came around. He has been completely alone since his parents died.

As for his dog, she has always had a

special connection to canines. Even those that did not like or trust people in general.

She glances out the window as she prepares the coffee pot, looks like it is going to be another nice cool day. The cool front came through during the night. The weatherman was actually right this time!

There was a little rain, but the sun is out now. She thinks she might just need a sweater to sit out on the porch this morning.

As she enjoys her coffee, Sam lays on the porch keeping an eye on things. Sam perks up with every sound. He is looking for Charlie to come into the yard. But no visitor this morning.

As she sips her coffee, her thoughts keep going back and forth as to if she should visit Reuben Schmidt. She finally decides to go for a visit him, after all what could it hurt.

She is still thinking he is just a lonely old man. Maybe no one goes to visit him because of all the stories that have been passed around this small community.

Emma has learned one thing after living here for ten years, a small town is full of talk. Each story seems to start out simply and truthfully enough. But as it is told and retold everyone seems to add their own embellishments to it.

Eventually most start to believe the stories with all the additional half-truths added in. To the point it becomes hard to remember exactly what the original story was.

Since she is not too sure about this man or his dog she does proceed with caution. She steps out of her vehicle and is greeted by a large, barking German Shepard.

She knows that she cannot show fear, she

stands her ground as he approaches. He is beautiful dog, and she can tell he is well taken care of.

Emma talks to him with German commands, telling him 'Sitz', the dog immediately responds and sits down. She smiles and tells him 'Platz', and again, he responds by laying down.

She then slowly and cautiously reaches to pat him on the head, and he begins wagging his tail.

"Well, you are not so ferocious are you."

Reuben Schmidt is quietly watching from the front porch as she walks up the front walkway.

He startles her when he says in a gruff voice, "If my dog likes ya, ya must be okay, but who the heck are ya?"

She introduces herself and tells him that a friend told her that he collects old books and newspapers. He slowly nods his head. She goes on to tell him that she has found a small part of a newsprint from 1953 and is wondering if by some chance he might have a copy of that newspaper.

She hands him the piece of paper Dash had found. She notices that he seems a little surprised when he looks at it.

He slowly gets up from his old rocking chair, using an old, scarred wooden walking cane.

"Well don't just stand there, come on in."

She cautiously follows the old man into the house, noticing that the years have taken a toll, as he limps slowly into the house with the help of his old wooden cane.

To anyone else entering his house it would look like a hoarder's paradise, but he seems to know exactly where to look to find that publication! He turns with the newspaper in hand, then hesitantly hands it to Emma.

She calmly asks if he would mind if she took it to the library to make a copy, she will be more than glad to bring it back today.

She promises to take care of the old paper, but he waves her off.

"Keep the dang thing, I ain't got no use for it anymore."

Emma is not expecting that from him, she carefully tucks it into her backpack and thanks him for his time.

As she turns to leave, she hears him mutter, "Ain't got much more of that left."

She gets into her SUV, assuming to herself he was referring to 'not much time left on earth'.

Driving home, she realizes that she was right, he is just a lonely old man, and his dog is his only companion. Maybe he prefers it that way.

As for his house looking spooky, it is just weather worn. It has not had a coat of paint in who knows how long, if ever. She might just find an excuse to go back to visit with him.

Mr. Schmidt might have some interesting stories to share. She gets the feeling that he does not trust anyone. She will have to work on building that between them.

As well as a good relationship with his dog. Since Mr. Schmidt seems to trust the dog's judgement of people.

After leaving Reuben's she goes to the library to let Mary know that she now has a copy of the whole newspaper for November 1953.

Turns out the date was the fourth of November, which means that the man had gone missing around the twentieth of October of that year.

Emma suddenly realizes __________ how was it that Rueben knew exactly which newspaper edition to get? The small piece she handed him did not have the full date on it.

Reading over the article they discover that the gentleman's name was Benjamin Louis Thomas _________ B.L.T.!

Could it be his pocket watch that Charlie had brought to her?! Had the old hat belonged to him?

When she arrives home, she gives Alex a call to tell him about her day, and about her visit with Reuben. She tells him that even though he may be eccentric, he is just a lonely old man that has spent most, if not all of his adult life to himself.

His German Shepard's name is Max, and he liked her too. At the other end of the phone, Alex shakes his head.

"Why doesn't that surprise me. I don't know of any dogs that don't like you."

Emma laughs, "Reuben said that I must be okay if Max liked me."

She tells him about the copy of the newspaper and the article. How Reuben knew exactly which newspaper to give her. How did he know the exact date?

"Is it just a coincidence that the missing man and the pocket watch have the same initials, or has Charlie uncovered the watch that belonged to Benjamin Thomas?"

Alex tells her to not get too excited over the discovery; it can all just be a big coincidence. She tells him to take care and she will talk to him later. She shakes her head as she hits the end call button on her cell phone.

"He is always the pessimist, maybe it is just his training and life as an officer for all these years."

As she says this aloud, Sam obviously thinks she is talking to him as he perks his ears up and wags his tail.

It dawns on her that she has not really given much thought _________ where did Dash get that piece of newsprint stuck to his paw? He never wonders far from home. Maybe she should take a little hike around their house and see if she can find anything else, maybe more of the newsprint.

"The next time I have to take Charlie home, I will take a little hike. I am sure the dogs will go for the exercise."

Besides anytime she can get in a hike she does it for the exercise. Plus, the chance to be outside and get some fresh air is always invigorating and seems to clear her thoughts.

Who was B.L.T. a.k.a. Benjamin Louis Thomas? If in fact, they are one in the same.

Emma tries Google but comes up with nothing. She knows it is a stretch, but she calls Tim and asks him if he had ever heard the name. After all he did grow up around this area.

Following a brief silence, he tells her he does not recall ever hearing that name. She does a search of the last several census records released, which are for the years 1920 – 1950. There is only one Thomas listed, on the 1930 census. It is a John Lewis Thomas, age twenty-seven, along with a son, name not listed, age seven. Could it be Benjamin's father? There is no wife listed.

Emma thinks maybe she had passed away. After all there were so many illnesses back then.

She decides to take a break from the laptop and refresh her cup of coffee. As she is heading out of the kitchen, Sam begins to bark at the back door. She knows that excited bark all too well, Charlie is outside.

When she opens the door, sure enough Charlie is standing on the porch. He drops an object on the ground, and he and Sam take off running and playing in the yard.

Emma picks it up and sees the handle of a small knife. It is in what appears to be a leather scabbard.

He has obviously dug it up somewhere. It is covered in dirt and what looks like greenish colored mildew. She gets a baggie, puts the knife in it, and goes into the kitchen to wash her hands.

After putting Sam inside and locking up the house, she loads Charlie up and heads to the coffee shop. They go around to the patio, where Tim meets them with a cup of coffee for Emma and a bowl of water for the dog.

"Do you have a minute? I have something I need you to look at."

Tim sits down at the table as she pulls out the baggie and shows him the small knife. She asks if he can clean it up since he has leather working supplies at home. He looks at it as he turns the baggie over.

"I can't promise anything, but I will try to when we get home."

Pointing at Charlie, "Let me guess, he brought it to you."

Emma smiles and nods her head as she picks up her backpack. Tim tells her he can stay with him. He will take him over to the bait shop. She tells Tim she will talk to them later.

After Tim and Shelby finish dinner, he

gets out his leather working supplies and begins cleaning the leather scabbard. As he starts to get some of the dirt and mildew off, he realizes it is hand made.

In the middle of cleaning up the kitchen Tim calls for Shelby to come into the living room. She turns the faucet off and dries her hands as she walks into the room.

He shows her that as he cleaned the leather, initials are revealed on the back of it. She asks him if these are the same initials that her mom had found on the pocket watch.

"I think it is, but I am not real sure."

He calls Emma and tells her about the initials he has found, B.L.T. She confirms they are the same ones on the watch. She thanks him and tells him that she will pick it up at the shop tomorrow.

After hanging up she thinks about it having the same initials. She is certain that with the dirt and mildew on the leather that Charlie had to have found it in the same area as the stock tank.

If these items belonged to Benjamin Thomas, and he went missing sixty-seven years ago, why are they showing up now?

The curiosity is getting the better of her, she decides to take a little drive the next day and pay a visit to Reuben. Maybe he knew who Benjamin was he has lived in the area his whole life.

Although she has been told by many, he is not too personable she is learning he is the complete opposite. At least he is when she goes to visit him.

Today, when she arrives, he invites her to stay for a cup of tea. She gladly accepts thinking he will share memories he might have of the missing person.

As he begins to reminisce of the days of growing up around the lake, she asks if it is okay if she takes notes of his stories.

He looks at her with a raised eyebrow, a little weary of why she would want to do this. Emma notices his skepticism and explains that she just likes history.

She likes learning of the area's past since she has only lived here ten years. Knowing that he also enjoys historical events, books, and documents, she is hoping her explanation will convince him to feel more comfortable with her.

He contemplates her reasoning for a few minutes and nods his head in agreement. She reaches into her backpack and gets out her notepad and pencil. As she opens her notepad Max comes over and lays beside her.

Reuben smiles, "He really likes you."

Emma reaches down and pets Max, "I really like him too."

Rueben begins telling her of growing up in such a small rural area, it was even smaller back when he was a kid. Although there was a small general store, a feed store, and the café. Later, after he grew up there was even a small-town lawyer.

He tells her how his family did not have a lot of money, but they always had fresh fish from the lake, venison in the winter and his mother always had a garden.

"I was an only child, my mother could not have any more, so I helped out as much as I could. I helped with the garden, cleaning up around here, and fixin' things that got broke."

Emma picks up on him saying 'around here'. She asks if he means this house.

"Yes, I have lived right here all of my life. Of course, with nobody else but me, it became mine when they died. My mother died when I was fifteen. I thought about dropping out of school. But it was very important to my mom that I finish high school. With my dad working out in west Texas, it was up to me to take care of this place and do my schoolwork."

He continued to tell of how his mother also took in laundry and did ironing for other people. When she had an overabundance of vegetables, she would preserve them and sell what she could.

"My father, Emmitt, traveled to west Texas for work, but would come home every month or so. He sent money home to my mother whenever he got paid. He finally had to stop working when his eyesight started to fail. He was only forty-five, he died when I was twenty-three."

When he pauses in his story telling, she quickly asks about the article she had read and if he remembers anything about the man that went missing in 1953.

"Oh, you mean Benjamin. I knew him well! When he was reported missing, the Sheriff's Deputy, Steven Whitaker, came and asked a few questions and that was where it ended. The story you read was the only report ever made, that I recall."

He goes on to tell her "Deputy said they would be investigating it. They marked it up to Benjamin just leaving town and not telling anyone. As far as I know that is where it ended. I never heard of anyone hearing from him or seeing him again."

She thanks him for the tea and tells him she will not take up anymore of his time.

As she puts her notepad back in her backpack and gets up to leave Reuben tells her, "Come back by anytime."

For whatever reason he likes Emma, maybe it is because his dog Max likes her. She has been told he never has any visitors and does not want any, at least until she came along.

It is just that people heard stories and never bothered to approach him. Max walks with her out to the gate, she pets him before closing it.

Since she has noticed that he does not have a car, she turns before getting in hers.

"If you need anything just give me a call. I will be glad to bring it to you."

As she is driving home, she realizes that he does not seem to have a television, at least not in that living room. But who knows maybe it is behind all those stacks of books and newspapers.

She did notice an old radio up on a shelf, maybe that is all he needs, or wants.

Then it dawns on her, she wonders if he even has a phone to call her or anyone.

Before heading on to her house, she stops off at Tim and Shelby's to pick up the knife, which Tim placed in a clean baggie for her. She lets them know how her visit with Reuben went. That he even invited her for a cup of tea.

Tim looks puzzled, "That doesn't fit all the things I always heard about him."

Emma explains how she thinks it is because his dog liked her on her first visit. Tim asks her how she won that Shepard over? He has heard that he is mean.

Emma laughs and explains, it came to her from having a German Shepard that was trained in German.

"I took a chance and spoke German commands to him, and that is all it took."

Emma goes on to tell them about the

stories he shared of his life, "He even remembered the Deputy's name that investigated when Benjamin Thomas was reported missing."

They are both surprised at the fact that he even shared all his memories of growing up. Let alone the story of Benjamin going missing and invited her back to visit.

Shelby thinks to herself, her mom was right. He is just a lonely old man that has lived alone all of his adult life. Nobody ever took the time to stop and visit with him. Of course, the dog did not like anyone else.

As she starts to leave, she tells them she will be heading into White Rock in the morning to pay a visit to Alex. She has one of her gut feelings that Benjamin Louis Thomas did not just leave town and move on.

Shelby just rolls her eyes at her

mom, knowing she will not let this go until she solves the question of 'What happened to Benjamin Thomas?', whoever he was.

After arriving home and letting Sam outside she fixes a glass of tea. As soon as she goes out on the porch Sam comes bounding up the steps to greet her.

She sits down on the swing to enjoy the sunset as Sam lays down at her feet. She cannot help but think about the conversation she had with Reuben earlier in the day.

The items that Charlie has shown up with have to be connected to Benjamin Thomas, somehow. She still finds it surprising that he invited her to stop by anytime.

Emma reaches down to pet Sam and picks up her book she has been reading. It is time to relax for a little while before Sam decides it is time to go inside and eat. You would think this dog had a watch and can tell time.

Sam abruptly wakes her up early, wanting to go outside. She sleepily slips on her house shoes and lets him out. She shivers and quickly closes the door. It is chilly this morning, too cool to sit outside.

She goes to put on a pot of coffee and lights the logs in the fireplace. While the coffee is brewing, she goes in and washes her face and gets dressed.

Ready for the day to start she fills her mug and heads over to her favorite over-sized chair next to the fireplace. Emma always loves the first fire of the season.

She decides to let Sam back in before getting on her laptop. He always has a way of wanting inside just as she gets occupied with working on her website or book.

She realizes as fast as time passes it will

soon be time for Tim to shut down the bait shop for the season. Matter of fact, it is just one more week before he closes.

After finishing her coffee, she grabs her keys and backpack along with Sam's leash. As soon as he sees it in her hand, he realizes he is getting to go somewhere.

"Since it is nice weather, you can ride along with me to go see Alex."

Before she can get down the steps he is already sitting next to the car.

When they arrive, she puts Sam's leash on, grabs her backpack and they head into Detective Day's office.

Of course, Sam gets a greeting before she does. She sits down and Sam takes his spot next to her chair.

She begins to tell Alex about her visit to

see Reuben and the stories he shared with her. How she was right, he is just lonely being by himself all these years. People really should not put so much weight into old stories passed around.

She pulls out the baggie with the old knife in it and points out that it has the same initials as the pocket watch.

She leaves the watch and knife with Alex, maybe he can find out more information about them.

As she takes Sam's leash in her hand and picks up her backpack Alex tells her, "Just be careful around that old German man. He is very eccentric and has lived alone his entire adult life. Just remember Emma he doesn't like anyone coming around his place."

Emma thinks to herself as she leaves, 'for whatever reason, no one except me'.

Alex sits back down at his desk and wonders why Mr. Schmidt has befriended Emma. She was right, he was just lonely, and the right person approached him.

After all she was a C.N.A. and has a way with elderly people. They seem to immediately take up with her.

She and Sam stop off at a drive thru to get a drink and a bite to eat. Sam knows the smell and knows he will be getting his favorite treat, french fries!

She drives over to the dog park. After eating she lets Sam run around for a little while before heading for Pinewood. There is just one other pup at the dog park, and Sam immediately starts playing with him.

After getting on the road for home, Sam falls asleep in the passenger seat. Emma smiles at him, he is a good travel buddy. As well as being her best friend.

Sam does not wake up until she pulls in the driveway at home. As soon as she lets him out of the vehicle he immediately runs over and grabs his toy and starts running around the yard.

"I guess you got your energy back sleeping all the way home."

A week and a half have passed when Charlie comes to visit, bringing Emma a new surprise. He drops it at her feet, and she sees that it is an incredibly old, leather man's wallet.

What drives him to dig up these things and bring them to her? The main question ___________ Why her? Why not Tim or Shelby?

He knows Emma will take an interest in it, and will see it as he does, something valuable. She gets a baggie to put it in, she will check it out later.

But first, she needs to take Charlie home. On the drive he begins to paw at her shoulder. She realizes it is by the wooded area where the stock tank is, the same spot he has brought her too before.

He immediately leads her to a large pine tree near the pond and starts nosing around at the ground. Emma checks out the area but does not discover anything other than a small animal skull, bleached white by the sun. Obviously, it has been here a while.

Charlie shows no interest in it, and in fact just stands by her, not interested in much of anything in the area.

He just wants her to know where he found his latest treasure. She calls for him and heads back to her vehicle, he jumps up into the backseat for his 'taxi' ride home.

As she opens the back door for Charlie to get out, Dash approaches them, barking and fussing at him for taking off again.

Emma asks Dash where his favorite ball is, and he takes off around the corner of the house.

When he comes back, it is not his ball he

has in his mouth! He as an old rolled up piece of paper in his mouth and drops it at her feet.

She carefully unrolls it, it appears to be some type of old deed, faded and dirty. Looking at Dash she asks him where he found this __________ he takes off around the house again. Emma follows him, but when he turns to greet her all he has is his baseball in his mouth.

So much for him leading her to where he found these papers. He drops his ball at her feet, and she throws it a few times for him before leaving.

She tells them she will see them later, points at Charlie and tells him to stay at home.

She decides to stop off at the library to show Mary the old deed, if in fact that is what the piece of paper is. If it is, maybe Mary can help her figure out what it is and where it might have come from.

They unroll it, realizing there is a signature at the bottom, but it is illegible. Mary does however confirm that it appears to be a deed to some piece of property.

She suggests that Emma might try taking it to the Courthouse. See if they might be able to help her figure out what it pertains to. They might even have a copy that would show the signature and to whom it belongs.

After arriving home, she lets Sam outside and texts Shelby to let her know she dropped Charlie off at home a little while ago, again.

After she fixes Sam's dog food, she puts a slice of leftover pizza in the microwave and calls Sam in to eat. As she eats her slice of pizza it comes to mind that she has the old wallet to check out.

She puts her plate in the sink and retrieves the wallet from her backpack. Sitting back down at the dining table she opens it very slowly and carefully. There is not much left in it.

There is only a couple of old faded dollar bills no driver's license, or identification of any kind. And no initials. Could this also have belonged to Benjamin?

Emma realizes that Sam is sitting at the door waiting for her to open it. She puts the wallet back in the baggie, and heads outside with him.

He takes off running around the yard as Emma laughs at how silly he is being since the weather has gotten cooler. She lets him play for a little while and then calls him.

"Sam, come on, time to go inside."

They share the couch and throw blanket as she finds something on the television to watch.

Not much is on, except a rerun of *Murder She Wrote.* Seems as good as anything else to watch. When it is over, she gets the book she is reading and wakes Sam up.

"Come on boy, lets head to bed."

She locks the door, turns off the lights and television, and with Sam right beside her they head off to the bedroom.

The next morning Emma drives over to White Rock and goes to the courthouse. Hopefully, she can find out where the property is located that is referenced on the old deed.

With some assistance from a very helpful elderly lady who works in the office they locate the property's description and coordinates.

They look it up on the map, Emma is surprised when she sees the location.

She immediately realizes it is the property where Charlie has been taking her. Including the Indian mounds and tank. The current owner listed is Reuben Schmidt!

Her first thought is where did Dash find this? He might have found it in the wooded area next to Tim and Shelby's property. It is possible that it was blown into that area by the wind.

That would be a far distance for it to be carried, depending of course on where it came from.

If it had been carried by the wind, would it have remained rolled up?

Why would an old deed be left out in the woods? Seems that it should be in a safe place in the possession of whoever owns it. Which from what it says, is Reuben.

As she starts to drive back to Pinewood, she considers going by to visit Reuben and see if he can answer her questions. But she is not sure about bringing this up to him.

She feels that she accomplished a lot just getting him to tell her stories of his past and about Benjamin.

She does not want to press their 'friendship', if that is what it is becoming. He seems to trust her now, and she does not want to jeopardize that.

It is still puzzling where it came from and how Dash ended up finding it. It is all she can think about. Different scenarios go through her mind. But with each one she finds a reason to dismiss it. She may never figure out where it came from, or how it got there.

After leaving the courthouse she decides to stop by to visit with Alex before heading home. He is just leaving his office when she walks up.

"I was just leaving to go get a bite to eat would you like to join me?"

Emma agrees to join him for lunch, while at the restaurant she tells him about the latest discoveries. The deputies name that Reuben remembered investigating the disappearance of Benjamin.

The old wallet, and the land deed. Along with what she found out at the courthouse, that it currently belongs to Reuben.

"Could it all be connected somehow to the missing man?"

"It might be, there isn't much I can do to help out. I can check and see if the deputy that investigated the disappearance is still around."

The officer would have long since retired, but maybe Alex can locate him. If he is still living.

She heads for home wondering if it is all just a coincidence. The items that Charlie has brought her, the papers that Dash has discovered and Reuben owning the property.

She stops off at the coffee shop. Pulling into the parking lot she is glad to see there is only one other vehicle. Shelby will be able to visit for a few minutes.

Shelby sees her mom pulling up to park and fixes her one of her favorite flavored coffees. Along with a slice of sopapilla cheesecake. Somehow, she knows her mom has more to tell her about Charlie's latest visits.

Emma tells her about the latest item he brought her, the old man's wallet.

"I checked it out, but there was no identification in it, just a couple of old faded dollar bills."

Then adds about the deed that Dash found somewhere and what she found out at the courthouse. The property description and owner listed on the deed.

"Alex is going to try to locate the deputy that investigated the missing person report."

Shelby knows her mom too well; she obviously is continuing her search. She will not just mark it up to the dog out digging and finding random objects. She did not expect Dash to be involved, it has always just been Charlie.

She also knows telling her mom that it is all just a coincidence will do no good. Her mom will not stop until she has figured it out.

Shelby knows all she and Tim can do is listen and let her go on trying to solve it. Her mom's little 'investigations' are usually interesting to some degree.

There is never any telling what she and Charlie might find. Besides writing her books, it does keep her busy.

Emma carries her cup and plate inside to the counter and tells Shelby she will talk to them later. It is time to get home and take care of Sam and relax for a while.

As she walks up on her porch, her cell phone rings. She pulls it out of her pocket and sees that it is Alex.

She answers it as she sets her backpack down and sits down on the porch swing.

"I have located the deputy, but I am not sure if he can be of any help. He now lives in a nursing home located in *Waco*. He has been living there for about six years."

He goes on to tell her he does not know the extent of his condition or why he moved there in the first place.

Sam, hearing Emma's voice begins barking and howling.

"I just got home and have to let Sam out, but thanks so much for calling me and for helping locate the deputy."

She sets her phone on the swing and goes in to fix a glass of tea and let the barking dog outside.

She grabs her laptop on her way out the door, she needs to check her email since it has been a couple of days.

It has been a long day, and it is time to just relax and watch the sunset. She shuts down her laptop and lays it aside.

As she watches Sam play in the yard, she cannot help but wonder if the retired Deputy can be of any help. At least Alex was able to locate where he is, and that he is still living.

She will look up the nursing home in *Waco* tomorrow and see what she can find out about Deputy Steven Whitaker.

She makes a note to herself to organize the list of items that Charlie and Dash have found. And add to that list the information she has found out so far, which really is not very much.

She still thinks there is more to this than Benjamin Thomas just leaving town without notification to anyone. Hopefully, the retired Deputy can shine some light on the investigation, if his memory is still good.

After having a cup of coffee and getting her thoughts together, she sits down at the kitchen table. Emma starts making a list, starting with what Charlie has brought her, and the papers that Dash found.

She then adds the information she has found out about each item, along with questions. She still wonders how Reuben knew what edition of the newspaper to get without her telling him the date.

She makes notes about Benjamin Thomas, which all she really knows is that he went missing.

She lays it aside and does a google search to find out the number and location for the nursing home in *Waco*.

She makes the call and asks if there are any specific visitation hours, she would like to visit Mr. Whitaker. The Nurse on the other end tells Emma that she would be welcome anytime. She also informs Emma that Mr. Whitaker does not have many visitors.

She goes on to tell her not to be too surprised at how he might react to her. He has been diagnosed with the beginning stages of dementia.

Well, it might not be a highly informative visit. But she makes plans to drive over to *Waco* this coming Friday.

She goes ahead and makes a hotel reservation for the night. Then calls Shelby to see if she can take care of Sam.

Her daughter questions her making what might turn out to be a wasted trip. Emma tells her even if it is, she can get some Christmas shopping done while she is there. After all it has been a while since she got away for even an overnight trip.

Shelby tells her to be careful and call to let her know she arrives at the hotel safely. She does not worry too much about her mom taking time off by herself. It is only a few hours' drive, and she has been known to drive across the country on her own.

Shelby smiles and thinks, 'that must be where I get my independence from.'

Emma packs an overnight bag and makes sure her phone and laptop chargers are in the backpack. She sets both bags on the coffee table, where Sam immediately checks them out.

As Emma heads to the kitchen, "Sorry buddy, you can't go this time. Shelby will come take care of you."

He goes to the kitchen as soon as he hears Emma fixing his bowl. She makes herself a sandwich and goes to the couch. After Sam finishes eating, she puts her plate in the sink and lets him outside. While he is out in the yard she makes sure she has everything packed that she will need.

Sam barks at the door letting her know he is ready to come back in. He follows her around as she locks up, turns off the television and extra lights.

"Come on boy, it is time to go to bed and read for a bit. I will be getting up early in the morning."

Sam is laying up on the end of the bed before she can even change into her pajamas. She pats him as she pulls the comforter back and gets into bed.

After taking care of Sam and having a couple of cups of coffee, she decides it is time to head out. After putting her bags in the car Sam follows her back into the house.

He proceeds to lay on the couch _______ pouting. He knows she is going somewhere without him.

Emma hugs him and tells him, "Shelby will be by later, and I will only be gone until tomorrow."

She checks his water bowl and unplugs the coffee maker. Tells Sam bye as she grabs her backpack and heads out the door.

She stops off at the coffee shop for a cup to go, and thanks Shelby for watching out for Sam.

Shelby reminds her mom to call her later and let her know she arrived safely.

"I thought I was the mother _________ I will call you later." Shelby smiles at her as she heads out the door.

Emma stops in at John's gas station to top off her tank. John asks if she needs him to check her oil, but she assures him everything is good.

He grabs the squeegee and starts cleaning her windshield. She smiles as the thought crosses her mind that this is the only 'full service' station still in business.

She notices that John does not move as quickly as he used to. But then he did inherit the station from his father thirty years ago, when he was in his mid-thirties. From what she has heard, he started working here when he was fifteen.

It is beautiful weather for a drive, and there is no rush, since she will not be visiting the nursing home until in the morning. Along the way she stops off at a few charming antique and junk shops. Mostly just to look around but you never know what you might find. She laughs to herself, thinking about how Charlie brings her plenty of things.

As she arrives in *Waco*, she realizes she did not have any breakfast today. She decides to stop off for something to eat.

After enjoying a nice lunch at the big market downtown, she decides to check out the shops. The shops are quint and fun to look in, and she finds a few Christmas presents to purchase.

She heads on over to get checked in at the hotel. On the way there she stops in at a convenience store. She picks up a couple of drinks and snacks for later since she does not plan to go out after she checks in.

After getting settled in her room, Emma

gives Shelby a call letting her know she just checked in and had a nice drive over. They talk about her stops at a few places along the way and enjoying a late lunch. She tells her to give Sam a hug for her, she is just going to relax and get a little writing done this evening.

She arrives at the nursing home the next morning, making sure to get there after the residents had time to eat breakfast.

As she signs the visitor's log the nurse begins informing her of what she might encounter.

"I understand, I was once a Certified Nurse Assistant in a nursing home, and I worked with dementia patients."

Since the facility knew he would be having a visitor the nurse leads Emma out to the patio where he is enjoying the beautiful weather. She lets him know he has a visitor and introduces Emma.

Emma lets the nurse know that they will be okay and Mr. Whitaker smiles at her as the nurse walks away.

"She is so nosy, and a busy body."

Emma cannot help but smile at his remark as she sits down. She introduces herself to him and he takes her hand and tells her he is glad to have such a lovely guest.

Emma smiles warmly at Deputy Whitaker and asks if he would like something to drink. He says he is fine but does not understand why such a nice stranger has come to visit with him. He does not get many visitors since moving in here.

She explains that she is interested in any stories he might remember from when he was a deputy.

He smiles and looks off in the distance, Emma sits quietly wondering if he is going to remember or share any stories.

He begins reminiscing about his days as an officer, mostly incidents involving mischievous teenagers and pranks.

He remarks, "That was back in the day when parents actually raised their children and not with all the high-tech gadgets."

Without any coaxing on her part, he begins telling of a missing person, Benjamin Thomas 'if he remembers correctly.' He was called out to investigate it in 1956 _______ no, 1953.

He goes on to tell her there was no evidence that there was any foul play, he seemed to have just gotten in his car and left town. Nothing of any value was missing from his house.

"I was sent out there because I was young, twenty-two years old, a new deputy. They thought people would talk to me. I was married to Sarah Mills. Her sister, Hannah Wright owns the café. At that time, their parents owned it."

"No one I talked to seemed to know why he would just up and leave. He had grown up in the area around the lake. All those that knew him said he was nice, but shy and stayed to himself."

He tells of how all those that had known Benjamin did not seem to want to discuss his family background. Even though most had grown up with him. When it came to any questions about his family, they immediately did not have anything to say.

"I always felt there was more to the story, but with no evidence of any wrongdoing there was nothing left for me to do but file the case under missing persons."

He added, "After all we did not have all the gadgets they do now to try and help with an investigation."

Emma can sense that this case still bothers him to this day. Having the gut feeling that there is something more going on, but no evidence to prove anything.

They visited for a little while longer. He tells her that he moved in here after his wife died, about six years ago.

It was becoming harder for him to take care of himself and his house. He and Sarah never had any children, so moving into the nursing home seemed to be the best choice.

"They had to have some reason for me moving in here, so they say I have dementia. Far as I can tell, my memory is fine. They take good care of me here."

Emma tells him about moving to Pinewood ten years ago, and about her companion, Sam. He states he has always loved dogs.

She realizes he seems to be getting tired. She picks up her backpack and gets up to leave.

"Thank you for coming to see me, please come back again." She promises that she will come back.

As Emma passes by the nurse's station on the way out, she lets the nurse know that Mr. Whitaker was ready to come inside. As she leaves, the nurse assistant heads to the patio to bring him into his room.

As she is pushing his wheelchair she asks, "Did you have a nice visit?"

He nods his head. She then inquires as to what they talked about. He simply says 'stuff' and smiles. He knows she is just being nosy.

After leaving the nursing home Emma heads back to the hotel to gather up her things and check out.

Once that is taken care of, she decides it is time for some lunch and shopping before heading back home.

While enjoying a bite to eat she thinks of Mr. Whitaker. It turned out to be an interesting visit, even though he has been diagnosed with the onset of dementia. His mind seems to work fine, at least the memories of his time as a Deputy.

He has clear thoughts on the investigation into Benjamin Thomas going missing. It is interesting that he thinks there was more to it than just him leaving town.

It is time for a little early Christmas shopping and of course a stop at the hobby stores. An easy place to find gifts for Tim and Shelby. They both love doing varying crafts when they are not working.

The thought crosses her mind, they should have their Christmas decorations out now. She stops in at the pet store, to get Christmas presents for all the dogs, including Rueben's German Shepard.

When she finishes there, she checks the time, it is going on three o'clock. It is time to gas up and head back home.

It has been a lovely day. However, she cannot get her visit to the nursing home out of her mind as she drives home.

She figures it is about time for a visit with her friend Mary. She will go to the library in the morning. But for now, she is just ready to get home and see Sam.

After coffee and some morning playtime for Sam, she puts him in his fenced yard and heads to the library. As she approaches the counter Mary looks up.

"It's about time you came by, haven't heard from you in days."

Emma smiles and tells her she has been a little pre-occupied. She proceeds to tell Mary that after a visit to see Alex last week, he had called her. He had located the deputy. Of course, he has long since retired.

"Deputy Whitaker is now a resident at Redbird Nursing Home in *Waco* and has been there about six years."

She explains that she went for a visit and had gotten home last evening.

She and Mary discuss the conversation she had with the Deputy. And that he is Mrs.

Wright's brother-in-law. But she either cannot or does not want to go to visit him. Mary then asks the obvious question.

"Are you sure he remembers things correctly?"

Emma had told her he is there due to the onset of dementia. Emma assures her that from the conversation and the way he talked about it, his memory is fine.

"He even told me that when he moved in the nursing home, they had to have a reason for him being there. So, they said he has beginning stages of dementia. According to him, his memory is fine."

Before leaving the library, Emma tells her she thinks there is more to Benjamin going missing than what was reported at the time.

They say their goodbyes and Emma heads over to Brewin' n' Bakin'.

Mary shakes her head and smiles. She knows her friend will not give up until she figures out what happened to Benjamin Thomas.

She has seen her get on the trail of an unsolved puzzle before. Thinking to herself, 'of course I find it just as interesting, especially when she needs my assistance'.

Mary thinks maybe she should suggest that Emma write a mystery. She has practice at solving them and they both love reading them. She shakes her head, nope she is meant to write books for children.

After stopping at the coffee shop and thanking Shelby for taking care of Sam she heads back home. She puts her things inside, fixes a glass of tea and grabs her laptop.

She settles on the porch swing after letting Sam out of his fenced area. She checks her email and finalizes the book she has been working on, time to submit it to the publisher.

"Maybe I need to read it one more time. Oh, for Pete's sake _______ just hit the submit button."

She gets it submitted, "Now it will be published and available for Christmas sales."

Sam wags his tail and puts his head by her leg. He always seems to understand when she is talking to him. She pats his head. He is a good companion to have around.

She decides it might be a good idea for another visit to the courthouse. A little more research into the deed that Dash found might turn up something interesting. The last time she was there she found out that the land is currently owned by Reuben. But she wonders if it had always been in his family.

The next morning, she lets Sam back inside, grabs her backpack and heads to White Rock. The same lady is working behind the desk and greets Emma with a friendly smile.

"Back to do a little more research today?"

Emma tells her that she is, but she knows where to look this time. She reads the deed and discovers that the land had been in the Schmidt family for several generations. The current owner is listed as Reuben Schmidt, dated 1954.

The owner prior to him is Benjamin Thomas! It was listed that he became the owner in 1950.

Just three years prior to him going missing. It had passed from Rueben's father to Rueben, then to Benjamin Thomas.

The land somehow became Reuben's one year after Benjamin was gone. She immediately wonders if there is a connection between Benjamin taking ownership and coming up missing shortly afterwards.

It is time for some internet research, but she can do that at home. Before leaving she asks if she can get a copy of the deed and is told that copies cost a dollar for each page. She hands her a dollar.

"I just need one copy of this page."

Driving home she has so many thoughts going through her mind. Maybe the internet can provide her with some more information on Reuben's family. At least it is worth a try.

After arriving home, she decides it has been a full day. She feeds Sam and makes herself some dinner.

It is time for some down time. She and Sam get on the couch and snuggle up to watch a movie. Halfway through it, Sam is snoring, and she is getting sleepy.

Sam gets the hint when she turns off the television and extra lights. He gets down off the couch, stretches and follows her to the bedroom. It is time for bed.

Sam snuggles up next to her as she puts her glasses on and picks up her book to read for a little while. Maybe getting lost in her book will push the rest of the things discovered to the back of her mind.

She settles in but before long she is dozing off. She wakes up with her book laying on her chest. She takes her glasses off, places her book on the nightstand and turns off the lamp. She notices the clock shows a little after midnight. She pulls the comforter up and quickly falls back to sleep.

Emma decides that since it is such beautiful weather this morning, she will take her laptop and go work at the coffee shop. She will be sitting on the patio so Sam can go with her.

He gets excited when he sees her grab his halter and leash. He gets even more excited when he realizes they are headed for the patio at the coffee shop. He knows Shelby will give him treats.

Tim walks over from the bait shop and joins her for lunch. As they enjoy a sandwich and chips he asks if she has found out anything more about the missing man.

She proceeds to tell him about the conversation with the retired deputy, and how she did not even ask, he just told her about his investigation.

"He thinks there is more to it than Benjamin just leaving town and not telling anyone. He is Mrs. Wright's brother-in-law."

She tells him about the information she found at the courthouse, about the property listed on the deed that Dash had found.

"Charlie has not been to visit lately, I am sure it is time for him to come over, at least for playtime with his buddy Sam."

Tim tells her Charlie has been coming to the bait shop with him as he has been getting it ready for the winter. Since he closed a week ago, he has been making sure everything is weatherproof, and that the heaters work properly. He must keep the bait minnows alive. He has been helping Shelby here at the coffee shop too.

They both say how they cannot believe it will be winter soon. Emma smiles and points out that before long the holidays will be here.

Tim cringes knowing that it means Emma will be unpacking her snowmen for the winter season. He teases her about how she really should check into Snowman Anonymous!

"I only have a little less than 300. I have to admit, I bought three new ones the other day, when I was over at *Waco.*"

They both laugh as Tim heads back over to the bait shop and Emma packs up her laptop to head for home.

She puts her things in the house and decides she needs a break from all of this. She opts for a walk with Sam.

After their three-mile hike he runs to his bowls in the kitchen and sits down. She gets the hint. It is time for dinner. She fills his bowls and fixes herself a bowl of soup.

After she finishes cleaning up, they go into the living room. She lights her scented candles, grabs her throw blanket, and settles on the couch with Sam.

As he dozes off, she begins to read the latest book she checked out at the library.

The weather has changed as they predicted, this morning is cool and rainy. She lets Sam outside, but it is not long before he is at the back door wanting back in. She lets him in and dries him off with the towel she keeps by the door.

"You know you are a dog, right? You won't melt."

She gets her backpack and cup of coffee and goes to the dining room table. She takes out her notes and studies them to see if there is a link between all of it.

Surely all of this is more than just a coincidence to Benjamin Thomas going missing all those years ago. It is just a matter of fitting the puzzle pieces together. Eventually they will fall into place.

The more she reads them and looks at

the items that Charlie and Dash discovered she gets a gut feeling that all of this is tied to Benjamin.

But how does the change of property ownership link into all of this?

The rain has slacked off when she hears a tapping at her back door, it must be Charlie, he has not been to visit in a week or so. She knows how he loves water, so instead of letting a wet dog in, she and Sam join him on the porch.

Charlie has brought her another surprise, it is a bone, sun bleached white, and dirt caked on parts of it. She gets a paper towel to pick it up with and puts it into a paper sack.

She wipes Sam's paws off and puts him in the house. Then she slips on her mud boots, just in case. She spreads an old blanket on the backseat and Charlie jumps in. The rain has stopped, and the clouds are starting to move out.

He paws at her shoulder at the same area where the pond is located. She takes a walk around the pond and wooded area but does not find any more bones or anything else for that matter.

She calls for him to get in and takes him home. She calls Shelby on the way back to her house.

"Just curious, did you give the dogs a large bone?"

Shelby tells her they have not given the dogs any bones in a while. Emma explains that Charlie showed up with a bone. A large bone, she guesses that he must have dug it up somewhere. Shelby tells her that maybe it is one that he buried to hide from Dash.

"By the way, I just dropped him off at your house. Will talk to y'all later."

When she arrives back home, she calls Alex and tells him about Charlie's latest discovery. She tells him she is not certain what type of bone it is.

"I will stop by after work and see if I can tell what it is from."

She puts on a fresh pot of coffee shortly before Alex arrives. At least maybe he can tell her what kind of bone it is and if there is any way to do any tests on it.

Once he gets to her house, she hands him a cup of coffee and gets the paper sack.

"I did not know what kind of bone it might be, so I handled it with a paper towel."

He chuckles at her for using a paper towel. He looks at it and says that even though he cannot be a hundred percent certain, but it does look to be a human bone.

"I will drop it off with my buddy at the lab and see if he can determine anything about it. It will not be a priority so it will be a few weeks before he finds out anything.

As he gets up to leave, he pats Sam on the head, tells Emma he will let her know as soon as he gets any information.

She thanks him for stopping by as she and Sam go inside.

"I am probably reading too much into this, surely it is not human. And even if it is, what are the odds that it belonged to Benjamin Thomas."

Emma has thought about visiting Reuben again. She is just not sure if it is a good idea to ask him about the land that was once his family's, then Benjamin's, and back to him.

She has a gut feeling that the piece of property changing hands and Benjamin Thomas going missing are tied together.

Maybe Mary can help her figure it out if they sit down and go over her notes and what has been found.

There must be some reason that Reuben did not mention the land. When she first asked him about the newspaper article, he stated that he knew Benjamin. But made it sound as if they were just acquaintances.

Of course, the bone that Charlie brought to her could be something other than human. But Alex even said he thought it was a human bone.

She will not know for sure for several weeks. He told her it would not be a priority for the lab. Emma thinks to herself that she is reading too much into all of this.

There must be some other way of learning what happened all those years ago with that land changing owners. But how to find out? It has been seventy years.

She takes out her notebook to make notes on ways of finding out. Adding to the list anyone she might be able to talk to, that lived here back then. And adding the bone found to the list of items Charlie has brought her.

The smell of the fresh pot of coffee gets her attention. She goes to fix a cup and heads out on the porch with Sam, with her notebook in hand. He has been patiently laying at her feet waiting to go outside and play.

She enjoys her coffee while Sam plays in the yard with his old stuffed duck. She loves watching him pitch it in the air and catch it.

When he gets tired of playing with his toys he will come up on the porch and lay down under the porch swing.

It is time to start making a rough draft of the new book she had an idea for. Maybe she can get it published shortly after the new year.

As she starts writing she thinks, 'I must be old school since all my first rough drafts are handwritten'.

It crosses her mind that it has been a couple of weeks since Charlie brought her any trinkets. As she is making notes, Sam lets out a high-pitched bark and goes to the top of the steps wagging his tail. She looks up to see Charlie coming up to the porch.

Does this dog know when she is thinking about him? Charlie always seems to show up just when she is thinking he has not been here in a while. He has just come for a visit this time and does not have anything to give her.

The dogs play for a few hours as she works on her new book. They stop for some water, and both come up and lay on the porch.

She decides to take Charlie back by the wooded area on her way to take him home. Maybe he will lead her to something of interest.

She calls Sam into the house, grabs her keys, backpack, and loads Charlie into the backseat. As usual he paws her shoulder as soon as she gets close to the same spot.

This time she decides to take a few pictures of the area where he had dug at the pond and the base of the pine tree.

It does come in handy having a cell phone with you, since it provides a camera wherever you might be.

After taking a few pictures around the tree and pond, she walks around the area to see if she discovers anything else that might be of interest. She comes up empty handed and heads back to her SUV, calls for Charlie to get in and takes him home.

As soon as she arrives back home she uploads the pictures to her laptop. As she looks through them, she sees something white at the base of a nearby tree. She had not noticed that when she was taking the pictures.

She enlarges it to get a better look at what appears to be part of a bone sticking out of the dirt. She prints it off and takes another look at it.

Looking at the picture she thinks she might be taking a drive over to White Rock but decides to go by the library first.

Emma tells Mary about the bone that Charlie brought her and then shows her the picture she took. Mary takes a long look at it. She gets up and gets her magnifying glass from behind the counter. She studies the picture again.

"It is really hard to tell what it might be. I can't say for sure that it is a bone. It could just be some type of reflection or a piece of trash or something else."

"I'm going to email it to Alex, see what he thinks. He probably thinks I am crazy for all of this."

They both laugh as Emma picks up her backpack to head home.

She emails the picture to Alex, then calls to make sure he received it. She cannot wait to get his opinion of what it could be.

After looking at the picture, he guesses it could be a small portion of a bone. But he is thinking more along the lines of a piece of trash or something other than a bone. He does not seem to show too much interest.

"You are not going to go out there and dig it up? Are you?"

She assures him that she is not going to do any digging. Charlie does enough of that for them both.

She decides to call Mary after a while, maybe she has some idea of how to find out what occurred with the land changing hands, without going to see Reuben.

Being Thursday Emma knows it is not a busy day for the library. Instead of calling she will just drive up there. Mary looks up and smiles as Emma nears the counter.

"Twice in the same day? What's up?"

Emma looks around and since no one else is in the library she suggests that Mary join her at a table. She pulls out the copy of the deed that she got at the courthouse. After she hands it to Mary, she tells her she is wondering how to figure out what happened with the land changing owners.

Without asking Reuben, she has a suspicion that whatever it was caused problems.

With a quizzical look, Mary asks, "Is there anyone else around here that might know what happened back then?"

The only person Emma can think of that is still around is Mrs. Wright, she owns the café. There is also John, he grew up around here, as well as his dad. He might have been too young, but he might have heard stories from his dad.

The only other person she can think of is the lady that helped her at the courthouse, she looks to be in her eighties, there might be an off chance that she would remember something.

On another subject, Mary asks if Emma really thinks it could be a human bone and if so, could it belong to Benjamin?

She tells her she is not for certain, but it came from the same area that Charlie took her to before, when he found other objects. So, it does have some significance.

"Kind of creepy, huh?"

Mary nods in agreement, "What if that

poor man has been buried out there all these years?"

Emma had not really considered that, and if it turns out to be him, what will be done with his remains?

After all these years, will they just be left there, or will someone give him a proper burial. She is sure he does not have any living relatives.

Oh well, guess we will cross that bridge when we come to it.

As Emma is leaving the library, Reuben's German Shepard comes running up to her. She finds it very strange since the dog never leaves Reuben's. When she opens the door of her SUV the dog jumps in her car, whining.

She drives over to the bait shop to see if Tim is free to follow her to take the dog home. She tells him something is wrong.

"Max never leaves Reuben's."

Since the bait shop is closed and Tim is not busy, he agrees to follow her out there.

"Let me tell Shelby I'm going with you out there to Reuben's."

They pull up in front of Reuben's house, Max starts pawing at the door and barking to get out.

Emma lets the dog out and closes the car door. As she turns around, she sees Reuben laying in the front yard.

Emma calls to Tim, "Let me get Max inside before you get out, call for an ambulance."

Emma calls Max and coaxes him inside the house. She then goes to Reuben's side as Tim joins her, he is on his phone giving the address.

She checks his pulse, it is weak, and his breathing is shallow, but he is alive. Where he is laying it appears that he fell coming down his front steps. She looks around for his cane and sees it a couple of feet away from where he is laying.

They hear the sirens off in the distance and Emma leans down and tells Reuben, "It will be okay. The ambulance will be here in just a minute."

As soon as they pull up the paramedics grab their gear, they hesitate at the gate. Emma notices it and tells them the dog is inside.

They start checking his vital signs and they get him hooked up to oxygen. They ask if she is family, Emma shakes her head no and tells them as far as she knows he does not have any living relatives.

After getting him on to the gurney, the paramedic tells her they will be transporting him to White Rock Regional Hospital, he has suffered a stroke.

"Do you know if he has a Do Not Resuscitate?"

Again, she tells them she really does not know, she has not known him that long.

As they pull away, Emma tells Tim he can go ahead and head back, she is just going to put some food and water down for Max and close the house.

After Tim leaves, she finds her way to the kitchen, locates some bowls, and gives Max some food and water.

She notices that he has a doggy door out of the kitchen leading into a side yard that is fenced. At least he can go outside on his own until she returns in the morning.

Once home, she lets Sam outside, and fixes his dinner bowl and her a bite to eat. She decides she will call the hospital after she gets through cleaning up her dinner dishes and letting Sam back outside.

When the emergency room nurse answers the phone, Emma explains who she is and that she is calling to check on Mr. Schmidt.

The nurse tells her that from what the paramedics said she thought Emma might be calling.

"We normally cannot give patient information out. Unless it is immediate family member. But I am sure under these conditions it will be all right to tell you.

Mr. Schmidt will be staying in the hospital for at least for a few days, it has been determined that he suffered a major stroke. He is resting comfortably now."

The nurse asks if Emma knows of any arrangements he has made in case of something like this happening.

"Not that I know of or that he ever spoke about, but I will check and let you know."

After she hangs up, she figures she will need to go back there and check on his Shepard in the morning. It will not hurt to look around for any documents he might have.

Emma arrives at Reuben's and Max is more than happy to see her. She lets him out to run, but he immediately goes to where Reuben had fallen. He sniffs the ground and whines. He then returns to Emma and stays close by her side.

Emma pets him for a few minutes, "It will be okay Max, I'll take good care of you while Reuben is away."

She heads inside looks around, shaking her head at the stacks and stacks of old books, newspapers, and magazines. From the date of the newspaper, he gave her he has been collecting since at least 1953. Probably for way more years than that.

She really did not pay much attention to the house the previous evening. She makes her way through the stacks and back to the kitchen so she can get Max some food and fresh water.

After he is taken care of, she stands there with her hands on her hips.

"Where do I start to look? Where would he even keep documents?"

She sees the top of an old roll top desk over on the other side of the room. It is barely visible for all the clutter. She figures it will be a good place to start looking. At least as good a place as any.

She makes her way through the stacks and rolls up the desktop. Which surprisingly rolls up easily.

There are envelopes and papers in the desk. Most appear to be faded and yellowed from time, and then she sees a legal size manilla envelope that looks new.

When she opens it, she discovers a handwritten will and letter-sized envelope with Mr. Whitaker's name on the front. Why would there be a letter to the Deputy?

There is also a sheet of paper with a handwritten will. It is written on paper with a letterhead from a lawyer's office. She looks at the bottom of the page and sure enough it is notarized.

There are instructions that if the need should ever arise for hospitalization, the hospital is to contact the lawyer, who has full power of attorney.

If he should ever need to be placed in a nursing home, arrangements have been made and paid for in full at the Redbird Nursing Home.

The same nursing home she visited Mr. Whitaker at!

If it should concern his death, arrangements have been taken care of at the Magnum Funeral Home, which is in White Rock.

There is one other large envelope, faded and dusty, it obviously has not been opened in some time. She decides to take it with her and read it when she gets home.

She places the envelopes in her backpack, tells Max (who has been laying at her feet) to go outside. She lets him run around while she puts her bag in her vehicle. She pulls her cell phone out of her pocket and calls the hospital.

She asks to speak with someone in billing. As she waits to be connected Max comes back to the porch and sits next to her.

When her call is connected, she lets the woman know that she is calling regarding Mr. Reuben Schmidt. She informs her that she will need to contact the lawyer and gives her the phone number at the top of the letterhead. She thanks Emma for calling and lets her know she will take care of it.

She gets up, puts her phone back in her pocket and tells Max to come into the house. She checks his water bowl one more time before leaving.

"I will be back to check on you in the morning, be a good boy."

As she turns to leave, he lays down on his blanket in the kitchen. She knows he does not understand what is going on and why Reuben is not here. She pets him and gives him some attention before leaving.

After arriving home and fixing a glass of tea she sits down on the couch and pulls the papers from her backpack.

She carefully opens the old faded manilla envelope and gently pulls the papers out.

It is a signed copy of the deed to the property she and Charlie have been exploring. The same deed she got a copy of at the courthouse.

It assigns ownership to Mr. Benjamin Thomas, dated 1950, on the back are handwritten notes, 'It won't be his for long; He can't steal the land from my family; I'll make sure it comes back to the rightful owner'.

The ink is faded some, but it is all legible. Emma again thinks that all of the business with the property ties into Benjamin going missing.

There is another sheet of paper with a handwritten statement 'the property is being signed over to Benjamin Thomas as payment in full for _________ , most of it is faded to the point of being unreadable.

The only part of the date that can be made out is 'tober of 1950', but not the day. Underneath is another note, obviously written by Rueben, 'it won't be his for long'.

Along with these documents there is also a statement from a lawyer's office with the address in Pinewood. Obviously long since closed, there is no lawyer in town now.

It states that upon Mr. Thomas' death and/or property taxes going unpaid for one-year the land will automatically be turned back over to Reuben Schmidt.

She places the papers back in the envelope. Could the handwritten notes signify that Reuben was involved some way with Benjamin missing?

Emma decides to put it all in her backpack. She will sort this out tomorrow.

Surely, she must be reading more into it than is there.

She heads to the Brewin' n' Bakin', orders coffee and tells Shelby about the documents she has found. At some time in the past there was a lawyer's office here in Pinewood.

Shelby gives her mom a surprised look. She explains that when she bought the building for the coffee shop there were boxes of old files everywhere. They got moved up to the attic.

"I think they are still up there. We did not even look in them or pay much attention to them. We just moved them up to the attic figuring we would haul them off later."

She tells Tim she will be right back. They both immediately head up to the attic to search for the boxes. They locate them and realize that on the end of each box is a year and the lawyer's name, W. L. Marcus.

Emma begins moving boxes seeing if there is a box with the year 1950 on it.

She finally locates it as Shelby tells her she needs to go back downstairs. Emma simply waves her off as she takes the dust covered lid off the box.

She pulls the box over closer to the light and begins going through the files. Halfway through the box she comes across a file with Reuben's name on it.

She pulls it out and begins going through the documents, finding one that coincides with what she found in Reuben's desk.

It states that upon the death of Benjamin

Thomas or the property taxes going unpaid for one year the property will hereby be returned to Reuben Schmidt. Free and clear. It is signed by Reuben and witnessed by Edna M. Marcus. It also states that a copy is provided to Benjamin Thomas.

Emma wonders who Edna might have been. But she does know one person in town that might be able to tell her _________ Mrs. Wright.

She is in her late eighties and owns the café. She has lived here all her life. She tucks the file into her backpack, turns off the light and heads downstairs.

She tells Shelby she might have found something of interest, but she needs to talk to Mrs. Wright over at the café. Before Shelby can even say anything, her mom is out the door. Shelby looks over at Tim and shrugs her shoulders.

With it being almost two o'clock the café will not be terribly busy. As she enters, the little bell above the door rings. Mrs. Wright comes out of the kitchen drying her hands on her apron.

Her grey hair pulled back in a bun. She looks like what every grandmother should look like.

"What can I get ya?"

"I'll just have a glass of sweet tea, and a moment of your time if that is okay."

Mrs. Wright gets her tea and sits down at the lunch counter next to Emma. She explains that she has come across some information that showed that there was once a lawyer with an office here in Pinewood.

Mrs. Wright does not even have to think about it as she replies, "Yes, Mr. Marcus, he was a nice gentleman. His wife Edna was his secretary and file clerk. His office was located over where your daughter has the coffee shop now. He was not rich by any means; he just helped the locals with any legal papers or problems they might need assistance with. He even helped me with the paperwork when I inherited this café."

Well, without having to go into any details as to why she was asking, Mrs. Wright answered her questions concerning the lawyer. Or so she thought.

She refills Emma's glass and asks why the curiosity about him. Emma quickly explains.

"I have just been doing a little research into the history of the town since I have only lived here 10 years. I love history of small towns."

That satisfies her question, Emma pays for her tea and heads for home. Emma is sure

Sam will be ready to go outside for a bit. It will give her time to add to her notes about all of this.

The next morning Emma gathers up all the documents along with the letter to Mr. Whitaker, her laptop, notebook and puts them in her backpack. She throws some pajamas and a set of clothes in her weekend tote, just in case she needs them.

She stops off at the coffee shop to let Shelby know that she is headed to *Waco*. As she turns to leave, she tells Shelby, "I'll call you later to let you know if I'll be staying overnight."

"Be careful and don't worry I'll take care of Sam if you decide to stay over."

Emma arrives at the nursing home just after breakfast and signs in on the visitor's log. She heads out to the patio where Mr. Whitaker is again enjoying the fresh air. Emma asks if he remembers her, he states that of course he does.

Just as she starts to tell him why she is here, the nurse approaches. Before she can say anything, Emma tells her they are fine, and will enjoy their visit out here on the patio. The nurse raises an eyebrow, turns, and goes back inside.

"I told you she was a busy body."

They laugh and Emma tells him that long story short, due to Rueben Schmidt suffering a stroke that she came across an envelope in his desk with Mr. Whitaker's name on it.

She hands him the envelope, but he frowns and immediately hands it back to her. Emma looks a little surprised by this move.

"My glasses are in my room, will you please read the letter to me."

She takes the letter out of the envelope, unfolds it carefully and although the handwriting is obviously that of shaky hands she begins to read it.

The first page simply states that if Deputy Whitaker is no longer living then this letter really will not mean much.

"September 19, 2020

Deputy Whitaker,

I thought you would be the one sent out to investigate the disappearance of Benjamin Louis Thomas in 1953. Being the youngest officer on the force it was no surprise when you arrived.

He had already been missing for two weeks by the time someone realized it and notified the Sheriff's department.

When you arrived, you did not find anything out of place at his home, only that his vehicle was gone. After talking with some of the town folks, you decided that he had just up and left town for no reason and without telling anyone that he was leaving.

Nobody seemed to question that a twenty-six-year-old man would just up and run away from home. He had a respectable job over in White Rock, working at the sawmill.

I somehow thought that you would be back to ask more questions, but that did not happen.

Until Ms. Johnson showed up asking me about a copy of the newspaper dated November 1953. She was not even alive then, but obviously has become curious for some reason about a missing man named Benjamin. Somehow, I have the feeling she will not let it go and will continue to look into it.

If you are reading this letter, then something has happened to me, either illness or death. Either way I am not concerned with the outcome.

I just wanted you to know that had you done a more thorough investigation back then, you would have found that he did not just leave town.

He wronged my family's honor back in 1950. I swore to myself and my family's memory that I would get revenge.

Should the law ever want to open this back up, they will find his car at the bottom of the lake, near the area of the old wooden bridge.

Just so you know, that has always been the deepest part of the lake. I knew that the car would remain out of sight _________ forever.

Even though so many years have passed, there may come a time that an animal or person stumbles across my cousin's remains long ago buried out by the old Indian mounds. At the time I thought it was a good place, after all old bones are always being found there.

Yes, he was my cousin. We were two years apart in age, he was the older one.

Had Ms. Emma not become so curious, then all this information would have gone to my grave with me, and no one would have ever come to learn that I got my revenge and rightfully got the land returned to me that belonged to my family for over four generations.

Rueben Schmidtt'

Mr. Whitaker sits there in silence for a few moments before looking up at Emma.

"I had a gut feeling there was more to him going missing. I had no idea he was Reuben's cousin. No one even hinted at it back then when I investigated the case.

We only had a few sheriff's deputies back then and did not have the time or men to investigate it any further. There was not any evidence to continue investigating, so the case was filed away as missing person - unsolved."

As Emma stands to leave Mr. Whitaker thanks her for finally putting his mind at ease about it and invites her to come back and visit him again. She promises that she will come back for regular visits.

After leaving the nursing home, she decides to stop for a bite to eat and call Shelby. She lets her know she will not be staying overnight, so no need to check on Sam. She needs to take care of Max too.

She decides to stop off at the hospital and check on Reuben. The emergency room nurse she had spoken with before sends her up to the fourth floor where he has been moved.

When she gets to his floor, she inquires at the nurse's station as to his condition. They inform her that it has been a major stroke, he will be moved to the nursing home tomorrow.

"It will most likely be where he lives out the remainder of his life, however long that might be."

The nurse asks Emma if she knows his age.

"I believe he is in his late eighties."

The nurse sighs and tells her, "We found an old driver's license in his pants pocket."

Emma tells her that he has not driven in

years and does not even have a vehicle. The nurse commented that it was no wonder, it had expired in 1955.

"His birth date is listed as March 14, 1925! He is ninety-five years old."

As she gets into her vehicle, she sits there for a few minutes thinking about what has occurred today.

Since she is in White Rock, she decides to visit Alex. Before she can tell him about all the events that have been taking place, he says he has news for her.

"The bone I sent to the lab came back; it is human. They did not run any other tests on it since it is not relevant to any current cases under investigation."

"I know, and I know who's it is!"

He leans back in his chair with a puzzled look on his face. She begins telling him what has occurred since Reuben's dog had come and found her that day in the library parking lot. She describes the papers she found in his desk.

"I have just come from the hospital, he will be moved to the nursing home, which is completely paid for. Where he will live out the remainder of his life."

She explains to him about the letter he had written for Deputy Whitaker.

"Benjamin Thomas was Reuben's cousin! Benjamin's car is still in the lake, by the old wooden bridge."

"Remember how we thought he was in his late eighties? Well, the nurse at the hospital found an old driver's license in his pocket. His actual age is ninety-five."

Alex opens his desk drawer and lays the watch and knife on the top of his desk. There is no reason for him to keep them now. There is no purpose to be served by re-opening the case.

Emma sits quietly for a moment, "What will happen with Benjamin's remains? He has no living family to make a request."

Alex tells her, "With no relatives, and no on-going investigation, they will remain where they are. It is sad, but there is no reason for this to be re-opened."

She puts the knife and watch in her backpack and leaves his office. Heading for home, she cannot help but think of how sad it is that Benjamin will remain buried in the area of the pine tree.

As she is driving, she thinks she can purchase a small headstone, at least to mark the place.

What a day it has been. She is ready to get

back and take care of Max and get home to Sam.

She stops off at the coffee shop to let them know she is back and will be heading by Reuben's to take care of his dog before going home. She lets them know it has been a remarkably interesting day, with some unbelievable discoveries as well.

"I'll give y'all the details later, for now I'm going to take care of dogs and go home and relax."

As she is waiting for Max to eat and finish running around outside, she walks over and sits down at Reuben's desk, she notices an envelope in one of the small cubby holes that she had not seen before.

She pulls it out ________ the front of the envelope has her name on it! Under her name is a date, it is the day after her second visit with

Reuben. She holds the envelope for a moment, wondering what it holds inside.

She gently pulls the letter out of the envelope, adjusts the lamp, and begins to read it.

The first thing she notices is the letterhead. It names a lawyer with an address in White Rock. She realizes it is the same lawyer on his documents concerning his injury or death.

She cannot believe what is in the letter. It states that upon his death all his land, home and all his belongings will go to her! Along with the German Shepard, since she is the only person besides him that the dog has taken a liking too.

She sits there for a few minutes in shock, until it comes to her attention that Max is whining at the front door.

She lets him in and fixes his bowl of water in the kitchen. She finds him another old blanket to sleep on since it is supposed to be chilly tonight. Emma tells him she will be back to check on him in the morning.

She turns off the lamp on Reuben's desk and slides the envelope into her backpack. She looks around at all the stacks of books everywhere. Shakes her head, pats Max and heads to her SUV.

It has been almost two months since Charlie had first brought her the cap he found. She sits outside enjoying the cool morning and watching Sam run around the yard. She cannot help but think of what an interesting two months it has been.

She had not expected to uncover a sixty-seven-year-old murder over a piece of land. Involving two cousins no less. All due to Charlie bringing her items that he found.

She often wonders if he senses that they are connected to someone that was involved in some type of incident. It seems that once he finds something he continues to go back to the same area and finds other items. Let alone the papers that Dash found. It is still a mystery as to where he located those.

She figures that after coffee and going

to check on Max, she had better pay a visit to Mary, at the library. She has a lot to share with her, including what appears to be a murder from the past.

She is not going to believe the twists and turns that the events of the past month have taken. All beginning with the old cap Charlie found. Luckily, Mary should have time to visit.

As Emma approaches the counter Mary is standing there with her hands on her hips, and a raised eyebrow.

"It is about time. Did you forget where the library is?"

They both smile at each other, and Emma asks Mary to join her on one of the couches.

She begins telling Mary about the last time she was here at the library, when Reuben's dog showed up. Reuben ended up having a major stroke and he is being moved to the nursing home. She will have to contact the lawyer about the letter stating that all his possessions go to her. Mary sits there in awe of all the events that have occurred.

"Do you think that the letter is a legal document?"

Emma shrugs her shoulders, "As far as I can tell it is, but only the lawyer can confirm it."

They visit for a little while longer, discussing the dogs, and what she will do with the German Shepard.

Mary gets up to show her the latest books that have come into the library. Of course, Emma cannot resist and checks out three of the new titles.

"I need a quiet evening with a good book."

Mary tells her as she is leaving, "Any evening is relaxing when you have a good book to immerse yourself in."

After getting up and awake she calls the hospital and is told that he has been moved to the nursing home, the evening before.

She takes a deep breath and calls the nursing home. As the phone rings she feels in her heart that Reuben will not be coming back home.

She asks what hall he will be on, just wanting to ease her mind that he would not be on the same hall as Mr. Whitaker.

It then occurs to her, that really is not a problem since Reuben is most likely bedbound, and Mr. Whitaker must use a wheelchair.

The nurse informs her, "Due to his condition from the stroke he will be placed on the hospice care hall."

Emma knows all too well what this means, he will not be around much longer.

After talking to the nursing home, she realizes she needs to get ready and go check on Max.

He is happy to see her as he has been since she started looking after him. She fixes him a bowl of food and fresh water. Emma lets him outside to run for a while as she sits on the steps of the front porch.

Sitting there it occurs to her that when Reuben passes on, this old house, the contents, the dog _______ will be hers! If the paperwork is legal.

She will have to introduce him and Sam and see if they can get along. What will she do with all the books, newspapers, and magazines? She shakes her head. She is letting her mind run wild.

After letting Max back in the house, she turns to go and notices a key hanging by the front door………it is the key to the front lock. Not that it really needs to be locked after all there is a guard dog in the house. He does not like too many people.

With all the stories that have been passed around all these years, she is sure no one is going to try to mess with anything.

Before returning home, she stops off at Brewin' n' Bakin', luckily the breakfast crowd has gone on to work. Shelby can sit down with her and have a cup of coffee. As well as telling her the wild story about the past week's events.

Emma can see the shock on Shelby's face as she tells her about the letter to the Deputy. Even more so when she explains that Rueben and Benjamin were cousins.

Emma goes on to tell Shelby about the letter to her about inheriting all of his possessions including the German Shepard.

After arriving home, she lets Sam outside, and fixes herself a bite to eat. She refills her glass of tea and goes to sit on the porch swing.

It is time to relax for a little while. She decides to work on her new book, until she goes back to check on Max this evening.

She thinks to herself, 'I pray that Max and Sam get along. It will be much easier to take care of Max if he is living here with her'.

After a few cups of coffee, she gets dressed for the day. She decides that after she goes to take care of Max, she will just relax the rest of the day.

What better way to spend a nice cool Saturday morning than on the porch swing?

She does need to contact the lawyer on the letterhead, Mr. Jamison. To see if it is a legal document.

She can at least look up the address online and see where he is located in White Rock. She will call him Monday morning.

She also needs to search and see if Reuben has any living relatives, after all she is not kin. If there is a relative, it would be a cousin or other distant family member. But they would deserve to inherit his belongings. She does not find anything that helps on the internet.

"Perhaps the lawyer knows if there are any living relatives."

She puts her notebook away, takes her laptop inside and calls Sam to come in. She curls up on the couch, watches a movie, reads for a little while and just spends the rest of the day relaxing.

She heads over and takes care of Max, then home for dinner for Sam and herself.

Monday morning, she calls the lawyer's office and requests an appointment to come meet with him. When the secretary asks what it is pertaining to, she hesitates a minute and then tells her it is regarding a client, Mr. Reuben Schmidt.

She immediately tells Emma she can come in at two this afternoon. Emma hangs up thinking that the secretary's quick answer was a little on the strange side.

Emma stops by the library to tell Mary about the call to the lawyer's office.

"His secretary seemed a little on the anxious side when I told her it was regarding Reuben. She immediately set up the appointment."

Mary shrugs her shoulders, "Maybe they were expecting you to call with all that has happened."

Emma nods in agreement. They visit for a little while until Emma checks the time. Mary wishes her luck as she heads out the door and gets on her way to the lawyer's office.

Since the library is not busy this afternoon Mary decides to do a little internet research on her own. Maybe she can find out if Reuben has any living relatives.

Emma arrives a few minutes before two o'clock. It is an older building in White Rock, but it is beautifully decorated inside.

She takes a seat, but only a few minutes pass before an older gentleman comes from the back and invites her to come with him.

Once in his office he introduces himself to her and asks what he can help her with.

Emma pulls the envelope out of her bag, and hands it to Mr. Jamison.

"I need to find out if this is a legal document."

Mr. Jamison looks over the paper and tells her, "Yes ma'am, it is all legal. I remember the day he called me and asked me to come to his house. He said he needed a will, of sorts, to be legalized."

He continues to tell her that he and his Junior Associate drove out there and witnessed it as Mr. Schmidt signed and dated it, making it legal and binding. The other signature below Reuben's is Mr. Jamison's associate.

She then explains how she has come to have possession of it, and that Reuben suffered a stroke and is now in the Redbird Nursing Home.

"Yes ma'am, I have taken care of his affairs for many years. I was contacted when he went in the hospital. Again, I was called when he was moved to Redbird."

"Does he have any living relatives?"

"No, that is why he wanted to leave his property and belongings to you. He said you were nice, and his dog likes you. He said he knew that you would take good care of Max."

She is in a bit of a daze as she drives back home. She goes by to check on Max and make sure he has food and water for the night.

After arriving home, she lets Sam outside

and calls Alex.

When he answers she asks, "Do you have a minute, well more than a minute."

He can sense something is wrong in her voice.

"Take all the time you need."

She begins by telling Alex that Reuben has been moved to the nursing home. She then explains to him about the envelope she found with her name on it. Emma informs him about her visit to the lawyer, and that it is a legal and binding document.

"For an old man that did not like anyone, he sure took a liking to you. When you do inherit all his property, what are you going to do with it?"

"I really don't know. If Sam and Max get along, I guess I will move him here to the house.

As far as the rest of it, it will take a while to sort through it.". When she gets off the phone Sam is waiting to come back inside.

Talking to Sam, as usual, "It is too late for lunch, and too early for dinner. Let's see what is on the television."

Sam curls up on the couch next to Emma until it is time for dinner.

It looks like it is going to be a nice fall day. Emma decides that after taking care of the dogs she will drive over to the nursing home and visit Reuben. She will also stop in to visit Mr. Whitaker for a few minutes.

She stops off at a florist near the nursing home. She figures she might as well take something to brighten up Reuben's room. She also picks up a little potted plant for Mr. Whitaker.

As she signs into the visitor's log she inquires as to what room Mr. Schmidt is in. The nurse looks at Emma with sympathy in her eyes.

"He is in Room forty-six on the hospice care hall."

Emma tells her that she called a couple of days ago and was told that he would be, she just did not know what room.

As she enters his room, the lights are dim. The Nurse Assistant is just pulling his cover back up when she notices Emma.

"I just finished repositioning him, we are trying to keep him as comfortable as possible."

Emma thanks her, "I understand, I used to be a Nurse Assistant."

As the girl leaves the room, Emma steps over next to his bed and places the fall arrangement on the bedside table. She pulls a chair up next to the bed and takes his hand.

Emma learned that the hearing is the last sense a person loses. She is not sure what he can understand, but she tells him that she has been taking good care of Max, and that they are getting along well.

She also tells him that she found the letter with her name on it, but she is not clear as to why he is leaving it all to her.

His lawyer did tell her that he has no living relatives.

"I will take care of the house. After I introduce Max to my dog Sam, I will move him in with us. I promise I will take good care of him. I say a prayer for your recovery every night, I do hope you get better."

Knowing in her heart that he will not recover. As she gets up to leave she feels him lightly squeeze her hand, which surprises her. She tells him, "I will be back to visit again."

She stops in the hall outside his room and leans against the wall for a moment, to get her senses about her. Another Nurse's Aide stops and asks if she is okay.

"I will be fine."

With a tear in her eyes, "Just please take good care of my friend."

The Aide assures her they will do their best.

Emma returns to the nurse's station to ask if by any chance Mr. Whitaker is enjoying the outdoors. She is told that he is and heads out to the patio. He perks up when he sees Emma approaching.

"How are you doing?"

"Much better now that you are here. What ya got there?"

"I just brought you a small potted plant for your room."

Emma smiles and tells him that she has been to see another resident. She tells him about Reuben being moved here, but probably will not recover.

She then explains to him about Reuben leaving all his property to her.

Mr. Whitaker has a look of surprise on his face.

"I am surprised that he left everything to you, but then he didn't have any relatives that I know of. He never liked anyone coming around. He just took a liking to you."

"It seems to be that he approves of me because his German Shepard likes me."

Mr. Whitaker laughs, "I remember that dog. When I went to ask him questions about the investigation into Benjamin missing, I didn't even get in the front gate. That dog did not like me at all. You must have a unique way with dogs."

Emma tells him she has always loved dogs. She tells him about working at the animal shelter before moving to Pinewood, volunteering mostly. They visit for a few more minutes and Emma leaves to head for home.

She sits in the parking lot for a few minutes pulling her thoughts together before driving back. So many things are going through her mind.

"I know he squeezed my hand, even if it was only slightly. Was he trying to tell me it will all be okay?"

Her cell phone rings just as she is walking up the steps of her porch. It is the Director of Nursing at the nursing home.

"I didn't know who to call. The only number I have is yours. I am sad to say that Mr. Schmidt passed away about thirty minutes ago."

Emma thanks her for calling and hangs up. She lets Sam outside and slowly sits down on the steps. He senses something is wrong and lays his head on her lap. She pets him as a tear rolls down her cheek.

"I'll will be okay, and you have a new brother dog that will come live with us, that is if y'all get along."

"What am I going to do with that house and all the stuff in it?"

As she sits on the steps thinking of the overwhelming job ahead of her, Sam paws at her arm. He does know when it is dinner time.

She wipes the tears from her cheeks and heads inside with him following closely. She fixes his bowl and cup of hot chocolate for herself.

She cannot help but wish she had met Reuben sooner. For whatever reason he had taken a liking to her. So much so that he is leaving all his property and belongings to her.

"I wonder what else I will come across as I go through his things and clear out the house.

How many other stories could he have shared with me?"

She will discover what it was that came between two cousins to the point of revenge. What could it have been that the property was used for 'payment in full'?

After letting Sam outside, and putting him in his fenced yard, she heads over to take care of Max. She makes sure he has fresh water and decides to take the key hanging by the front door. Not sure why, but she locks the door, and then heads to the coffee shop.

She lets Tim and Shelby know that she received a phone call informing her that Reuben had passed away.

Shelby takes Emma's hand in hers, "Mom I'm so sorry, but at least you got to visit him one last time."

Emma nods, "I guess the first thing I will have to do is see if Sam and Max get along."

As for the rest of it, she will just have to figure out where to start. She checks her watch. It is about time for the library to open. She tells them she will see them later, and heads over to talk to Mary.

Shelby turns to Tim, "This seems to have upset her more than I would have expected. It isn't like she had known him a long time. One thing is for sure, Mom never inherited property from solving any of her little puzzles."

Tim replies, "Along with a dog, sure hope for her sake that Max and Sam get along. And who knows how Max will take Charlie's visits."

She slowly approaches the counter just as Mary looks up. She immediately realizes that something is wrong, Emma is not acting herself this morning, and looks like she has been crying.

She tells Mary about Reuben as they go to sit on one of the couches. She hands Emma a tissue as a tear rolls down her cheek.

"Thank you, I'm not even sure why this has upset me so. I only knew him a few months,

I had only visited with him twice, three times if you count the nursing home.”

They talk about where she will start at his house. First, she will have to introduce the dogs. She then tells Mary about what a mess the house is in.

“Do you think you could go over there with me one day? You can help me sort through the books, who knows some of them might be worth something.”

Mary, without hesitation, tells her she would be glad to help her.

After arriving back home and letting Sam come up on the porch with her, she calls Alex. She tells him about Reuben and lets him know she might need his help.

“What an interesting individual he was. Who knew that he would take up with you the way he did? You were right, he was just lonely."

"I don't really know what all is in that house yet, but some of it might be antiques that may be worth something."

He tells her to just let him know ahead of time and he can take off one afternoon and come over.

Well, at least she has lined out some help. She still cannot get the thought out of her mind of what a task this is going to be. Now to call the Veterinarian over in White Rock and get an appointment for Max.

She does want to make sure he has all his shots and is in good health, even though he appears to be. Then she can make plans to introduce Sam and Max.

Emma wakes up early the next morning, she looks at her clock and sees that it is only six a.m. She has her coffee and lets Sam back inside, since it is chilly this morning, she will leave him inside. She heads over to take care of Max, as always, he greets her at the front door.

She kneels down and hugs him, as he licks her cheek. She gets up and heads to the kitchen.

After getting him fed and letting him outside for a little while, she calls him back in. It is time to head over to Tim and Shelby's for Thanksgiving dinner.

As she drives over she thinks to herself, 'I can't believe it is almost December. Where did this year go?'

Thinking it will just be the three of them, she is surprised to see other vehicles there.

Shelby decided to surprise her by inviting Alex and Mary for dinner. They both would have just been spending the day alone.

Shelby has prepared a wonderful dinner. They enjoy friendly conversation and coffee afterwards.

Tim and Alex talk about fishing, getting together next Spring. Emma and Mary make plans to meet at the coffee shop in the morning, and head to Reuben's.

When Alex and Mary leave, Emma thanks them for inviting her friends, it was an awesome surprise.

After arriving home, she lets Sam in the house and fixes him a special dinner with some of the leftovers Shelby sent home. She divides the leftovers giving half to Sam.

She puts the container by the door with the other leftovers in it. She will take some to

Max in a little while when she goes to feed him.

Both dogs enjoy their Thanksgiving treats. She hugs Max and tells him she will be back in the morning. He has a full belly and curls up on his blankets as she leaves.

After arriving back home, Emma sits on the swing, lost in thought. She thinks about Reuben and wishes she had gone to visit him long before she did.

It happened this way for a reason she does not understand. At least she saw him before he died. She believes in her heart that he knew she was there.

"Maybe he was telling me goodbye by squeezing my hand."

Her thoughts turn to Deputy Whitaker. The diagnosis of dementia. Yet his thoughts and memories are fine.

As she watches Sam play she is thankful she has him. She hopes that Max and Sam will be good buddies.

She calls Sam and heads inside to get ready for bed. Sam hops up on the bed and lays down. Emma climbs in bed and picks up her book to read for a bit.

As she gets comfortable and situates her pillows her thoughts turn to how thankful she is for all she is blessed with in her life.

Since it is Black Friday, Emma and Mary meet up at the coffee shop. They enjoy a cup of coffee and a piece of sopapilla cheesecake before heading over to Reuben's house.

Shelby and Tim are busy today with all the shoppers that have come into town to visit the small stores and antique shop. After finishing their coffee, Emma tells Shelby she will see them later.

Emma unlocks the front door flips on the lights and puts Max outside. When Mary enters the living room, she lets out a gasp.

"Oh my gosh, you were not exaggerating. This looks like a hoarder's paradise."

"Yes, but the strange thing was, Reuben seemed to know exactly where any given item was in here."

"When I asked him about that edition of the newspaper from 1953, he went straight to where it was."

Emma looks around, "I will start with his desk, and you can start with the books next to it. We will just work our way around the room."

Mary asks if she has even seen any of the rest of the house.

"Just this room and the kitchen actually. I have not even ventured any further."

They look at each other with curiosity, and slowly head down the hall.

The first door to the right is just a small bathroom, but surprisingly it is clean and well kept.

A little further down the hall there is a door to the left and one across the hall to the right. Both are bedrooms, again, they are clean, the beds are made, and only a little dust on things. The furniture and decorative items all appear to be antiques.

The last door off the hall must have been his room. Although the bed is made there is a stack of books on the bedside table.

Two small bookshelves are so full that books are stacked on top of them and in front on the floor.

Mary looks at a few of the books and realizes that they are incredibly old but in excellent shape. One of the books is even signed by the author and dated 1935.

Mary looks over at Emma, "He must have really liked to read. I can't believe how many books are in here. Not to mention all the ones in the living room."

Emma thinks again how she wishes she had come to meet Reuben sooner. He was bound to have more stories from his childhood and growing up here in this house.

Emma is surprised to see a small television on a table in the corner. There is also an old trunk at the foot of the bed. Looking at it and at each other, they decide to explore that later.

They head back outside to get the empty boxes from their vehicles and get started sorting through all the stacks of books and magazines and _______ his desk.

As Mary starts with the first stack of newspapers, Emma hesitantly sits down at the desk, and thinks to herself, 'I haven't sat here since Reuben was taken to the hospital'.

She sighs, as her thoughts about Reuben are interrupted when Mary asks if she is okay. She assures her that she is and takes a pile of papers from the top of the desk.

As she sorts through them, she finds most

of it is just junk mail. Underneath a pile of old papers, she has cleared off, she discovers an old photo album. She lays it with her backpack. She and Mary can look at it later.

After clearing the top of the desk, she begins sorting through papers and envelopes in the small cubby holes.

Mary continues going through magazines and newspapers, sorting those that might have any type of value into boxes. It crosses her mind that she might catalog some of the old newspapers for the library, just for historical purposes.

When she hears Emma gasp, she immediately steps over to the desk. Emma looks up at Mary with a shocked look on her face.

"Look what I just found!"

Mary takes the document and as she

reads it, realizes that it is a receipt of sorts, handwritten.

Emma tells Mary, "That is not Reuben's handwriting."

As Emma reads over it, she realizes it is a legible copy of the document she had found in the faded manilla envelope. This one is in better condition and shows the date as October 20, 1950.

It also states that the property is being signed over to Benjamin Thomas by Reuben Schmidt. It is payment in full for a debt owed by his father, Emmitt Schmidt to his uncle, John Thomas.

According to a letter that is with the document, which is typed, it is obvious that his uncle died before the debt could be repaid. It also states that the debt is to be paid to Benjamin Thomas as the sole heir to his father's affairs.

She turns it over to see if there are any notes written on the back, but there are none. Unlike the copy she found with threatening notes written by Reuben.

Emma places the document and letter back into the envelope and puts it in her backpack. Thinking to herself, 'I need to compare this with the old document I found'.

She continues going through papers that she finds in the cubby holes but finds nothing else of interest. After she finishes the cubby holes and cleaning off the desktop, she starts going through the drawers.

At the back of the top drawer there is a letter-sized envelope with her name on the front. She calls Mary over and shows her the new find.

"Well, open it!"

Emma pulls the letter out and begins to read it out loud.

"Dearest Emma,

If you are reading this, then I must be dead. I knew that you would find it though, you are a very curious girl.

I am sure that you have figured out that I left all my possessions, home, and land to you. And I know that you must be wondering why. You see I never married, never had any children, and Benjamin Thomas was my last living relative.

When you first came around, I was a little hesitant to talk to you. But I knew I could share my stories with you when Max took to you as soon as you got out of your car.

I was impressed when I heard you speak German to him. So, I guess you could say I left it to you because Max liked you, and I came to like you very much. Even though it was only a brief time of getting to know you, you came to feel like family. The family I never had.

I am sure you were told that I stayed to myself and to be careful approaching me. But you did not hesitate to talk to me, and I thank you for that.

Reuben Schmidt"

With tears in her eyes, she is only able to choke on her words.

"I was right, he was just a lonely elderly man living alone."

Mary hands her a tissue and tells her it is time to take a break from all of this.

"Let's get a bite to eat. It is not like this all must be done today. Besides, I have a box of old magazines and newspapers to go through.

That will keep me busy for a few days."

Emma smiles up at Mary and they gather up their things. As Mary puts the boxes in her car, Emma lets Max back inside and locks up the house.

She pets Max on the head and tells him she will be back later to fix his dinner. She follows Mary as they head to the café for some lunch.

As they enter the café, they realize it is already two o'clock, no wonder there is only a few customers here. Mrs. Wright approaches their table.

"What can I get you girls?"

They order sweet tea and BLT sandwiches. As Mrs. Wright heads for the kitchen, Mary starts laughing.

"How appropriate, BLT's _________ or maybe not so appropriate."

They both laugh and take time to relax and enjoy lunch. They keep their conversation on other things, besides Reuben.

Mary tells Emma how nice it was that Tim and Shelby invited her for Thanksgiving, and what a fun time she had. They discuss decorating for Christmas soon. Mary always goes all out at the library.

When Mrs. Wright brings their plates, she cannot help herself.

"I hear you inherited Mr. Reuben's property and dog."

Emma nods her head as she takes a bite of her sandwich. After she walks away, she tells Mary, "I guess everyone around here knows."

"Well, it is a small community and there is not much for them to do but keep up with what is going on with everyone else. I like the way you took a bite to avoid that conversation."

Again, they are laughing.

They finish their lunch and Mary heads to the library. She is eager to check out the box of magazines and old newspapers she brought from Rueben's. Emma tells her she will see her later and heads for home.

She opens the gate to the fenced yard and is met with barking and a wagging tail. She takes her things inside and comes back out to play with Sam for a few minutes. He continues to play as she pulls her phone out of her pocket and calls Alex.

He asks how she is doing, and she begins to tell him about the documents and the letter written to her, that she found today.

"So, he left you everything because his dog likes you?"

Emma just smiles, "It appears that way from the letter."

"I did not really find anything else interesting. Other than the original debt was between Reuben's father and his uncle. And I was right, there are a lot of antiques in that house."

"You didn't find anything saying what the debt was for?"

She tells him that is all she knows, unless she finds something else, she has not finished going through the desk drawers.

They say their goodbyes and she puts her phone in her pocket. She calls Sam to come inside and decides to go ahead and go feed Max.

After getting back home she fixes Sam's bowl and the coffee pot.

A warm cup of coffee and some down time sounds good. She can finish the current book she is reading.

While Sam eats, she gets a hot shower and changes into lounging pajamas. It has been another interesting day involving Reuben. She lets Sam outside and fixes a cup of coffee.

After letting Sam back in she could not help but to re-read the letter Reuben wrote to her. She thinks back to the first time she went to visit him.

How she had thought then that he was just lonely. Now, this letter he has written confirms that.

She thinks aloud. "You were his best and only friend it seems Max."

The thought comes to mind, 'things happen for a reason'. She takes a sip of coffee and wonders, what is the reason for this chain of events? Why does Charlie always bring what he finds to me? It is not as if solving this brought any justice to Benjamin being murdered.

However, it did give Mr. Whitaker closure to the investigation. Maybe that was the purpose of solving this puzzle.

Emma picks up the old photo album. She slowly and carefully begins to turn the pages.

On the fourth page are pictures of two young boys. On the back is written, 'Reuben and Benjamin, age 10 and 12'.

She looks at the picture again and realizes Benjamin is wearing a hat. The same type as Charlie had brought to her, could it be the same hat? There are several more pictures of the boys, and in each one, Benjamin is wearing his cap.

The last picture of the boys she looks at also has notes on the back. It reads, 'Reuben and Benjamin, ages 17 and 19, Benjamin's grandfather's pocket watch, Graduation'. She turns the photograph back over.

She goes to get her magnifying glass, and discovers he is holding a pocket watch! Apparently, the same pocket watch that Charlie found.

The remaining pictures are of Reuben and his parents. There are a few at different ages of Reuben and a German Shepard.

As she is putting the letter and the photo album on the table her phone rings, it is Shelby.

"Hi mom, I was just calling to see if you were okay since I hadn't heard from you after you left the shop this morning."

She tells Shelby about the documents and the letter she found. Describing to her how well the rest of his house was kept, except for the living room and kitchen. She tells her of the photo album. After they left Reuben's, she and

Mary had stopped at the café for a late lunch.

"Have you decided what you are going to do with the property and house?"

Emma replies, "Not yet, there is still a lot to go through and a lot of the furniture and décor in the bedrooms seem to be antiques. I will have to have someone appraise them."

They visit for a few more minutes and after hanging up Emma tells Sam, "Lets go to bed and read for a bit."

He follows her into the bedroom and is on the foot of the bed and laying down before she can kick off her house shoes. She grabs her glasses and book from the nightstand and snuggles in to read.

As she is reading the mystery, it dawns on her, maybe Mrs. Wright knew Reuben's parents or uncle. Seeing how it has always been a small community, and even smaller back then. She might have some information or at least a story giving her an idea of what happened between them.

It might even be worth talking to John. He might have heard stories from his dad. Having the only gas station, news was bound to pass through there.

If she can find out what the debt was, then she might know why it was so important to Reuben to get the land back that had belonged to his family.

She lays her glasses and book on the nightstand and tells Sam goodnight.

Although Emma does not eat breakfast very often, she decides to go to the café this morning. She pours a cup of coffee and lets Sam out. Since it is turning into a beautiful day she puts him in his fenced yard.

She gathers her things and heads over to check on Max.

She fills his bowls and gives him some attention. As she is petting him she tells him, "I'll be back later, and then you can go for a ride to the veterinarian and meet your new brother dog. I just hope y'all get along."

Since it is closer to brunch, the café is not terribly busy. Hopefully, Mrs. Wright will be able to visit with her for a few minutes.

When she arrives, there are only a few customers all seated at tables, she decides to take a seat at the counter.

Mrs. Wright greets her with a cup of coffee and takes her order for a breakfast plate. Emma figures she might as well go all the way; she adds biscuits and gravy to the order. It does not take long before Mrs. Wright brings her plate to her.

Emma thanks her, "Can you sit with me for a minute and visit? I have a question that I would like to ask you."

Mrs. Wright looks around the café.

"Sure, I can, I own the place."

"I was wondering if by any chance you knew Reuben's parents or his uncle. Since I have inherited his place, I was simply curious about his family."

Mrs. Wright thinks for a moment and then begins to tell Emma what she can remember.

"I know at one-point Rueben's father, Emmitt and his uncle, John Thomas were as close as brothers. There was not too often a time they were not seen together.

Then Rueben and Benjamin were always together, best of friends, all the way through high school.

They both graduated but were two years apart. As I recall it was especially important to Reuben's mother, who had died when he was young."

Mrs. Wright takes a sip of coffee and continues, "Benjamin graduated two years ahead of Reuben and got a job over in White Rock at the mill. Reuben just stayed to help his dad, even after graduation. By then his father was not able to work any longer.

Reuben and Benjamin had a falling out in

later years. It was handed down from their fathers. Then it carried on between Reuben and Benjamin. Those two boys were always playing or going fishing together, that is until their fathers had a parting of the ways."

She takes another sip of her coffee and then continues.

"Reuben's father was in debt to his uncle for quite a considerable sum, or so it was said. But his uncle died before it could be repaid. The sum of the debt was passed on to Benjamin to collect."

Mrs. Wright pauses for a moment in thought.

"I am trying to remember what the debt was for. I'll remember, just give me a little time."

She gets up from the stool and refreshes their coffee, and then checks on her other customers. In deep thought, she wipes the counter and clears Emma's plate. Without a word, she heads into the kitchen, leaving Emma to wonder if their visit is over. Suddenly she joins Emma and sits back down.

"I remember now. I was about twenty years old, but I remember my parents talking about it. It was an interesting conversation for such a small community. It was said that Reuben's uncle had tricked his father into signing over the property out where the Indian mounds are located."

She sips on her coffee for a minute, "It was to repay a debt for money his uncle had supposedly given or loaned to Reuben's father."

She went on to explain that after his uncle died, Benjamin would not let it go, he said he had rights to that property, but the only proof was what his father had left him in a letter.

Right before Reuben's dad died, he told him that it was all just a trick to get the property from the Schmidt's.

"From the talk that went around, it was said that Reuben's dad was a drinker back in the day. I figured the two men got to drinking and Reuben's uncle started the whole story of money changing hands. Which left him owing John, and eventually the land changing hands."

As they grew older, Reuben finally gave in, but he was smart enough to go through a lawyer. They drew up the paperwork that Emma had found in the desk.

Emma thanks Mrs. Wright for the information she has shared, pays for her breakfast and heads over to the library.

She tells Mary about the visit she had just had with Mrs. Wright. The story that she was told about Reuben and Benjamin, how close they were as boys. The debt between their fathers, passed down to them, which ended their friendship. Mary sits quietly for a moment.

"It is crazy that a piece of land could cause such dissension among family members. Carried on for years to the point of him committing murder to gain back possession of the land."

"Then leaving it all to me. What am I going to do with it? I am seriously thinking of selling it, with the history it has, I am not sure I want to keep it."

They visit for a little while as she shows

Mary the picture of the boys in the album. Emma points out the cap Benjamin has on, that it was the first item Charlie had brought her.

"Do you actually think it had belonged to Benjamin?"

"It sure looks like one and the same, he has it on in every picture in here."

Mary tells her she might have a collector interested in some of the old magazines and books. From the ones she has looked up so far, about half of them are worth some surprisingly good money.

As Emma drives to her house, the idea comes to her, the money from those old magazines and books will go to the library. Depending on how much they sell for, renovations and repairs can be done, as well as ordering new books. That will be a great surprise for Mary.

The money she gains from the sale of the land where the Indian mounds are located will be donated. She will just have to figure out what organization to give it to.

Talking to herself, "that is a clever idea, I just don't feel that I should benefit from any of it. Especially since a man was killed for it."

Emma decides it is as good a time as any to pick up Max and take him to the Vet's office. She goes by and picks him up and heads to White Rock. She just wants to make sure he has all his shots and is in good health.

As soon as the vet sees Max, he calls him by name. Come to find out Reuben used this vet too.

"May I ask why you are bringing him in."

Emma explains that Reuben had suffered a stroke and passed away, he had left Max in her care. She told him of the pictures she had found of Reuben as a young boy and through the years. In many of the pictures there was a German Shepard.

He informs Emma that Reuben had always had a German Shepard around and always took diligent care of them. He tells Emma that Max is seven years old and in very good health. He will not need his shots for another nine months.

After leaving White Rock she decides it is no better time than the present to introduce Sam and Max.

Introductions are made through the fence to begin with. Unbelievably, they immediately start wagging their tails, and playing through the fence. She decides to introduce them face to face, and they start playing.

Emma cannot believe that they have taken to each other like they have. She looks skyward.

"Reuben, did you have anything to do with these two getting along? Well, Max now has a home and a brother dog for as long as he lives."

She is in such a good mood, after deciding what to do with all the stuff at the house, and the Indian mound property. So thankful that the dogs get along so well. She decides it is time to decorate for Christmas.

She puts the dogs in the fenced in yard and heads to her storage building to start bringing in totes of decorations.

It has turned out to be a wonderful day, including the weather. She stacks the totes on the porch. After getting them all moved inside she calls the dogs to come in with her.

Max has to check out the totes as she opens them. He then loses interest and goes over and lays down with Sam.

As she enjoys a cup of coffee, she realizes it has been about a month since Reuben died, and she brought Max to live with her and Sam.

She is watching Sam and Max run and play in the yard, thankful that they get along so well.

From the first time Charlie showed up after Max joined her and Sam, they have gotten along well too.

Max has even come around to liking other people. He really likes Shelby and Tim. Of course, Tim plays with him every time they come over, and Shelby brings them treats.

Sitting on the porch swing enjoying her coffee, a thought comes to mind. She had concluded she did not want to benefit from the sale of the land or the house. So, instead of selling the property where the Indian mounds are, she will donate it to the community for use as a park. The money that comes from the antiques and other possessions, as well as the house will go to a fund to improve the park. And she will purchase a headstone in memory of Benjamin.

She smiles, pleased with this new idea, Mary will like this. Maybe Tim and Shelby can help with the design of the park.

That can be part of their Christmas surprise, telling them about her plans, and their part in developing a park.

Now if she can just keep it to herself for another week, until Christmas!

Christmas morning has dawned with a cold front coming through during the night. Emma lights a fire in the fireplace, lets the dogs outside, and starts a pot of coffee.

It is only a few minutes before the dogs are at the door wanting back inside. They both head to the kitchen for a drink of water.

After they get a drink they curl up in front of the fireplace as Emma sits on the couch with her coffee.

"Hey boys, I almost forgot, Santa came!"

They both perk up as she gets up to get their stockings down. She lays a stocking in front of each one and they immediately start investigating what is inside.

As they pull out their new toys, playtime commences. So much for a nice quiet Christmas morning in this house.

Her phone rings and she sees that it is Alex.

"Merry Christmas, just wanted to call and tell you that I hope you have a great day."

"Thank you, I hope you have a good day too. I'll be heading over to celebrate with Shelby and Tim about lunch time."

She tells him about her surprise for them, helping plan the park that she has decided to put in at the land she inherited from Reuben. Alex thinks it is a great idea.

He asks how the dogs are getting along. Emma tells him they are best of buddies, and Max even likes Charlie.

A few minutes after hanging up, her phone rings again. Shelby is calling to wish her a Merry Christmas and to see what time she will be over to their house. Emma tells her that she is just watching the dogs play with their new toys, and she will be there about noon. They talk for a few minutes before Shelby tells her that she has to get some cooking done.

After Christmas lunch, just the three of them gather in the living room to exchange gifts.

Shelby and Tim are both surprised when they open the card telling them about the park and the planning that they will help with. They both think it is an excellent idea, to have a park, with a walking trail.

Shelby winks at Tim, "We can discuss this more later, go ahead, open your present Mom."

As Tim places her present in front of her she cannot imagine what is in such a large package. She is overwhelmed when she gets the wrapping paper off and sees that it is a metal detector.

She has been wanting to get one, but just has not taken the time. Tim knew that she would like it.

As they visit for a while, she tells them she cannot wait to go out and use it. After she figures it out. Tim shakes his head.

"I'm betting that won't take you long to figure out."

Shelby adds, "We thought you would like it, especially going on your adventures with Charlie."

They all start laughing as Charlie perks his ears up when he hears his name. She gathers up her things, and heads home to spend the rest of Christmas day with the dogs. She plans on a quiet evening with the fireplace burning and watching a movie or two.

The week after Christmas Emma wakes up to a quiet and chilly morning. Sitting on the porch swing with her throw her thoughts turn to the idea for a park. She can name it in honor of Reuben. She turns her thoughts to all that she has done at Reuben's house.

Mary has sold a lot of the old books and magazines. She was so surprised at Christmas when Emma told her where the money from the sales would go, to the library.

As she takes a sip of coffee, it dawns on her that Charlie has not come to visit since before Christmas.

Startling her out of her thoughts, both dogs start barking and wagging their tails.

She looks up to see that it is Charlie coming up the walk _________ what does he have in his mouth!?

Acknowledgments

Trick and Rosco, the black lab and blue heeler, for being the inspiration for this book, as I continue to run the 'Trick Taxi' a couple of times a week, when he comes to visit. Rosco still stays home and waits for me to bring his 'brother' home, and fusses at him when he gets out of my car.

Sam (my Pittie mix} my foster-fail and my assistant 'editor', who sleeps on the job.

And Rolf, my German Shepard ________ who crossed the Rainbow Bridge on Father's Day 2022. He did not like many people, but he always kept an eye on me and was my protector. He was also bi-lingual, trained in English and German.

Lindsey Brown for being my sounding board and giving me ideas when I needed a little help. For always believing in me, and providing sopapilla cheesecake, just not often enough!

Brad D. for helping me to discover 'Rueben Schmidt', when I needed a name to fit an old eccentric gentleman. And for always being there when I needed a little help, from installing a television antenna to changing a flat tire.

About the Author

T. (Tami) Brown is a born and raised Texan, where she has lived all her life (except for the four years living in Pennsylvania). She earned an associate degree from Del Mar College in Corpus Christi, Texas. Where she excelled in English and English Honors.

She has always loved writing and had her own by-line in a small-town newspaper, "Elementary, My Dear".

She enjoys fishing (with the custom wrapped rod her dad made her), traveling _____ even if it is just a daytrip, and spending time writing. Which has kept her busy during the year (2020) of masks and quarantines.

She resides in the hill country of Central Texas with her canine companion, Sam and his two kitty 'sisters'.

Note from author:

You can visit my website where I post excerpts, introduce characters, and announce coming books in The Pinewood Mystery series. I also enjoy writing my blog entries, covering everything from writing to life.

I hope you enjoyed this book and look forward to the coming books in the series.

www.tbrown-author.com

I began this book in 2020, finishing this second edition in 2024. I took 2023 away from writing when my father passed away February 2023. By the time everything was finalized and taken care of it was October.

I am now returning to my love for writing. He was my biggest fan since the printing of my first book, From 'Nomex to Scrubs'.

I will be publishing second editions of the Pinewood Mystery series in 2024 – 2025. And I will be working on a new book I have rough notes for.